His hand tig

Susy laughed a[...]
why do we girls [...]

'Because you are so charmingly feminine, Susy, that's why!'

It was a diplomatic reply. Had Ross but known, it was nothing to do with her high heels or the gravel, but the touch of his hand grasping hers so firmly. And, with a sense of shock, the sudden unmistakable telltale tingle that ran through her fingers caught her unawares.

Dear Reader

This month we touch upon personal grief for the heroines in TROUBLED HEARTS by Christine Adams, and SUNLIGHT AND SHADOW by Frances Crowne, both handled with sensitivity. PARTNERS IN PRIDE by Drusilla Douglas and A TESTING TIME (set in Australia) by Meredith Webber give us heroines who are trying hard to make a fresh start in life, not always an easy thing to do — we think you'll both laugh and cry.

The Editor

Frances Crowne's nursing career was set aside for marriage and three children, yet left a sense of thwarted ambition. Later a secretarial career at an agricultural college was followed by freelance writing of romantic fiction and articles for women's magazines. A chance remark at a party led to her writing her first Medical Romance. Now woven with romance, her nursing ties have come full circle in a most gratifying way.

Recent titles by the same author:

LOVING QUEST
LOVE'S CASUALTIES

SUNLIGHT AND SHADOW

BY

FRANCES CROWNE

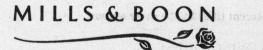

MILLS & BOON

MILLS & BOON LIMITED
ETON HOUSE, 18–24 PARADISE ROAD
RICHMOND, SURREY, TW9 1SR

First published in Great Britain 1994
by Mills & Boon Limited

© Frances Crowne 1994

Australian copyright 1994   Philippine copyright 1994
This edition 1994

ISBN 0 263 78603 X

Set in 10 on 11 pt Linotron Times
03-9406-59793

Typeset in Great Britain by Centracet, Cambridge
Made and printed in Great Britain

CHAPTER ONE

'Iт's no good, Dad, I'm finished with nursing, I've quite made up my mind, and that's that!'

Ian Frenais, tall and distinguished-looking swung the car away from Jersey airport that sunny afternoon in August, giving his daughter an affectionate glance but one which held a welter of hidden anxiety. Both he and his wife Dorothy had known of this state of affairs now for the past few months, and things had obviously not improved.

'Well, if you say so, my dear,' he answered in his quiet, firm voice, 'but, as we said on the phone last night, don't make any hasty decisions at present. Personally I think it's too soon.'

Susannah's dark brown eyes stared unhappily beyond the windscreen as they drove through the holiday bustle of St Helier, and out towards the countryside of the island she loved. A small inner sigh escaped her as she said limply, 'I know it's difficult for you to understand, Dad, but it's something I can hardly talk about even now.'

'I do understand, believe me, darling, but all we want you to do at present is to have a complete rest. After all, the sole reason you've been sent home from Belfast is to try and put everything behind you for a while. Working there for more than three years in the thick of the Troubles is enough for anyone, let alone losing Patrick so tragically.'

Susy, as she was known to her family and friends, bit her lip tensely, twisting the diamond engagement ring on her finger as her thoughts wandered to the night when they had exchanged rings and their marriage was just a week away. Nevertheless, the British Army still had its job to do, and the day before Patrick was due to go on leave to Jersey—where he and his relatives had arranged to stay—as a newly commissioned officer he was detailed to take a group of his men on patrol in the Falls Road. A suspicious-looking car had been parked in a side-street, Patrick went ahead on foot to examine it, it was booby-trapped and he was killed instantly.

From then on, Susy's life as a nursing sister in orthopaedics at the Belfast hospital slowly began to disintegrate, imperceptibly, at least to herself.

Now, as they climbed the cliff road towards St John's Bay, Susy's voice was tremulous. 'Well, Dad, at least I can face being home. Eighteen months ago I couldn't; leaving Ireland was like. . .like leaving Patrick alone.' Her lips quivered as she fought to regain control. 'Crazy, really.'

She shifted her gaze to the sea below, turquoise satin edged with cream lace like bridesmaids' gowns. . . Her father's comforting hand moved across to cover hers and the pressure between them said far more than words.

'We know what you're going through, Susy. And you mustn't forget that if there's anything your mother and I can do to help get you over this bad patch, you only have to say.'

'Thanks, Dad—you and Mum have been wonderful.' She gave her father a brilliant smile that transformed her neat features and full, sensitive mouth to a thing of beauty. 'Now, what about you two? We never had much time on our weekly phone sessions, did we? How is Senior Paediatric Consultant Frenais coping at the Jersey General? Still a shortage of staff, no doubt? Not forgetting his lovely wife, my mother, and her endless charity works?'

Her father chuckled. He was still a handsome man

in a studious, intellectual sort of way, she thought proudly, seeing the familiar long vertical laughter-lines appear down either side of his mouth like brackets.

'Much the same as ever, Susy. And you're too right about the staff shortage.' His voice had taken on the gentle lilt it often did when embarking upon a favourite subject, a legacy from his Scottish mother. 'However, I'm very glad to say that the new paediatric unit is almost near completion. A few finishing touches here and there, and the equipment will be installed next week, we hope. The formal opening will be held shortly. Did I mention in one of my letters that we've appointed a colleague, my junior paediatric consultant, Ross Beaumaris, to be in complete charge eventually?'

'Not that I remember. Has he been at the hospital long?'

'Long enough to know what's what. About five years. He's divorced—lives on the island here. Very nice chap, ultra-keen; work seems to be his life.'

'Sounds OK. You think he's the right man for the job?'

'Sure of it. Our ideas and plans run along the same lines. I want to know the place will be in good hands before I retire, and that won't be too long now.'

'Go on, Dad! You're only a young sprig of sixty-two. You'll keep the consultancy anyway, and nothing will lure you away from that.'

Ian Frenais grinned. 'I hope you're right, darling! The main thing now is to find some really good staff for the unit.'

'Will you leave this Ross. . . Beaumaris to appoint them?'

'Not entirely, no. I think he'd rely upon me if I recommend anyone. However, we're not worrying too much about that at the moment. Now what else was it? Oh, yes, your mother! Well, that's another story altogether! Lately she's been doing quite a lot for a local orphanage that takes only disabled children; she's really quite marvellous with them too. Needless to say she roped me in. I don't get a great deal of spare time, of course, but she's usually got a job or two lined up for me!'

'That sounds great, Dad. You know, you and Mum are super.'

Her father smiled at her, relieved that his daughter's thoughts had been diverted for a while. 'Shall I tell you something? We have a super daughter, too, and we'd better step on it now. I happen to know there was a great deal of extra-special cooking going on in the kitchen when I left earlier. . .'

At Rosebriar Lane, they turned into their driveway and stopped outside Rosebriar Cottage, a long, low two-storey house despite its name, its pink-washed walls ablaze with swatches of crimson climbing roses. On either side of the open front door stood tubs of mixed flowers, their perfume sending the bees to a frenzy.

Susy stepped from the car, sunlight finding the natural gold glints in her long brown hair, white jeans and buttercup-yellow T-shirt emphasising the tall, wand-like slenderness of her figure. 'Home. . .' she murmured wonderingly. 'How good it is to be here.'

Her father was at her side, flinging an affectionate arm around her shoulders. 'Welcome back, darling. You'll pick up from that wretched breakdown now, I just know it.'

A sudden rush of emotion caught Susy when from the side of the house her mother appeared looking as fit and well as ever, with short brown curly hair, her blue eyes lit with her usual lovely smile. The blue summer dress she wore brought a stab of nostalgia to Susy, remembering happy childhood summers. Even as her mother's arms enfolded her in that loving embrace, the bleakness of the past months overwhelmed her. . . 'Mum, oh, Mum. . .' she choked, burying her face in the warm softness of her mother's neck.

'Susy, my dear, words can't express. . .' The words stuck in her throat as she saw the sad, lost expression in her beloved daughter's face. 'You're home now, my love,' Dorothy said briskly, swallowing hard, 'and it's just wonderful.'

Talking as if they'd never been separated, they linked arms and went into the panelled entrance hall aromatic with roses and furniture polish, while her father collected the bags from the car. Ever practical, her mother got down to basics. 'Firstly a nice cup of tea for all of us, I think. It's all ready on the patio, Susy, I mustn't tire you with a lot of chatter; suffice it that you're here. We'll soon have some colour back in those cheeks. I'm sure you haven't been eating enough, and that's something I can improve upon!'

When later Susy went up to bed after a delicious meal and so much excitement, her tiredness seemed to evaporate and all she wanted was to be alone. Alone with thoughts of Patrick and their love that was to have lasted forever. . . Her bedroom had been newly decorated, items of furniture from teenage days gone; it had now become a very comfortable bedsitter. It would be so easy to slip down this inviting slope and spend the rest of her working days—whatever they might be—just returning to such a haven where every decision would be cushioned by the love of her parents. Not a bad prospect, she thought morosely; after all, what did life hold now?

She took a shower, then put on her dressing-gown and for several minutes gazed out of the open window where beyond the garden and the orchard lay a silver skein of sea. Her childhood memories returned again—of a childhood spent with her brother Graham, of happiness, fights and skirmishes, but followed by their

formative years of study which drew them together
again. He was twenty-seven now, two years older than
herself, and already a computer boffin in the USA.
Forging ahead, with breathtaking success. Not in quite
the way her father would have liked—his hopes for his
son had been in medicine—nevertheless, they were all
very proud of him.

Thinking about him drew her to his room, which
seemed to bring him closer. Photographs of cricket,
tennis, football, rowing teams, in all of which he
featured. There was a picture of herself on which she'd
written, 'To Brother Bunty, masses of love.' A silly
nickname but one that had clung. On his bookshelves
she spotted the copy of Palgrave's *Treasury of Poems*,
which she'd given him when he passed his A levels.
Leafing through it, stopping at a blank page to read his
boyish hand, she saw that he'd written:

> Beauty, strength, youth, are flowers but fading seen;
> Duty, faith, love, are roots, and ever green. . .
>   George Peel. 1558–97.

She re-read the telling lines several times over, then
slowly closed the book. An Elizabethan poet and
playwright had stirred up a like consciousness in
Graham's mind, it seemed, a reminder of the new life
before *him*. Shouldn't that apply to her also? Was it
right that she should think of giving up the job she
loved? Had she really lost all faith in herself and the
people around her? The roots of her upbringing were
as strong and firm as ever, yet she had known deep
troughs of despair, doubting everything and everyone
since Patrick died. His love had been a reality, though,
nothing would ever change that, and thinking now
along such lines could surely help make the rest of her
lifetime fall into some kind of perspective. . .

Thoughtfully she returned to her room, almost as if

Graham had tried to put her mind at rest, and within
minutes she was in bed and fast asleep.

Lazy days followed: days of leisure, of reminiscing with
her mother, of just drifting. Until one morning she
realised a whole fortnight had passed since she came
home, and, sitting in the kitchen as she was that
morning, it seemed the most natural thing in the world
to be helping her mother top and tail gooseberries
picked from the garden. Dorothy Frenais had just
made a cup of coffee and was saying lightly, 'Phew!
What a marvellous scorcher this morning, Susy. Are
you going for a swim?'

'No, Mum—too lazy, I think!' The radio was spilling
out cheery pop music, and Susy, relaxed in sun-top and
shorts, glanced with amazement at the large bowl of
golden-green fruit piled ever higher. 'Do you really
need all those, Mum? There's mountains of them!'

Dorothy smiled, amused to see her daughter aware
of things which a few years back she would have hardly
noticed. 'My dear child, they'll be jam shortly, and
we'll be selling it at one of my favourite garden fêtes!'
She put her head to one side suddenly. 'Was that a car
door I heard? Your father's taken to coming home
lately for coffee. . .'

Susy carried on snipping. 'Dad's jolly sensible. Your
brew's a darned sight better than anything they turn
out in hospital!'

'I could have been mistaken, I suppose,' her mother
still pondered, looking quite disappointed. 'Oh, well.'

'What's this I hear from Dad about your work with
disabled children, Mum?'

That really made her mother's eyes light up. 'I've
sort of adopted them all at the home with a few friends.
We have a rota, and each of us has six children whom
we hold in our charge specifically. We take them out

on set afternoons, quite often to our own homes, and generally make them feel one of the family.'

'Not all at once, I hope!'

'No, dear, we're well organised and. . .' Dorothy raised her head again. 'There! I was right, it's your father! I wonder who he's brought home this time. I'd better top up the coffee.'

Ian Frenais appeared at the kitchen doorway from the garden, a large beam on his face. 'Come along in, Ross!'

A tall, lean and athletic, dark-haired man, head and shoulders taller than her father, stepped into Susy's vision with complete assurance. Her mother welcomed both he and her father with her usual warmth. 'Ian! Ross! How nice to see you both! Ross, you must meet our daughter Susy; she's on extended leave at the moment. This is Ross Beaumaris, Susy. You know, the colleague who is working with Ian.'

Susy's first impression of the newcomer had been fleeting, but even so he certainly had presence with an almost elegantly agile grace, and seemed very aware of it, which showed in the easy manner with which he smiled at her. 'Hello, good to meet you.' The dark blue eyes and tanned features could have been those of a sailor; the rugged, tough look about him seemed in complete contrast to the requirements of his profession, his expensively cut suit rather belying his probable inclination for a bare torso and shorts while handling the sails of a yacht.

They shook hands, but not before she'd attempted to stand up to make room for him round the table, and to her embarrassment the heat of the morning was such that the tops of her legs stuck to the chair. She saw the laughter in his eyes as she managed to extricate herself while they released hands, making her feel like an overgrown schoolgirl. 'Morning, Doctor,' she muttered too formally, 'do sit down.'

Quite oblivious, while talking to Ian, Dorothy served more coffee, and Susy realised she was incapable of thinking what to say to this man at her side. It was he who said brightly, 'Ian tells me you're home from Belfast, Susy. It must have been rather tough going over there, particularly the nursing.'

She attempted a casual laugh, over-conscious of his understandable interest in her experiences, but too aware of his long-lashed eyes as she wondered just how much her father had told him. She purposely kept her reply vague. 'Oh, no more than any other stricken area, I don't think.'

An expression of sympathy touched his strong features, the aquiline nose, firm mouth and square chin revealing, she imagined, a stubborn trait perhaps indicative of his nature. He made a small grimace at her reply. 'Well, I hope you're going to be able to make up for a lot of lost time while you're here. Remember, today Jersey, tomorrow the world!'

She stayed for as long as politeness required, but was suddenly overcome with a deep sense of melancholy, as if another man showing an interest in her job resurrected the feeling of utter inadequacy which generated her need to escape those quizzical eyes, the crazy thought pounding through her mind that she saw one of Patrick's expressions there, making it even more essential that she leave immediately. When she did give her excuses, it seemed about as unsophisticated as when she'd stuck to the chair. Heaven knew what conclusion this man would draw about Ian Frenais's daughter! Susy only knew that she had handled the occasion with all the clumsiness of a galumphing elephant in a china shop.

Upstairs in her room she calmed down, trying to convince herself that she had made too much of the incident. And yet that moment of comparison with Patrick definitely unnerved her. Was this sort of thing

going to happen whenever she spoke to a stranger? She
had imagined she now had things under control, even
to steeling herself against certain music, especially the
slushy, romantic tunes she and Patrick had loved to
dance to, but she was totally unprepared for this newest
hurt. It seemed that memories still surfaced unexpectedly, catching one off guard. During her recovery
period from the breakdown she had been offered
counselling for delayed shock, but eventually she'd
insisted she was strong enough to see herself through
the blackness of mental despair. Now she was
unsure. . .

She bathed her face and changed into a cool sundress, brushed her hair and tied it back, feeling better
for the small discipline. Downstairs in the kitchen her
mother, alone now, was busy stirring the berries into a
large preserving pan. Susy put an arm around her
mother's shoulders. 'Sorry I was so unsociable earlier,
Mum. I'm not too good with strangers at the moment.'

Dorothy Frenais put aside the wooden spoon with
which she'd been stirring. 'Let's both sit down for a
minute, darling,' she said, pulling out two chairs.
'Look, you know we haven't said a great deal about
this whole business yet. You see, your father and I
thought it best that it should take its natural course.
You're here to recover, to find your old self again,
revitalise your body and your mind. At the same time
to come to terms with what's happened. Nothing can
be done in a hurry, and I certainly don't expect you to
apologise each time if you think these small steps
forward are not going quite as they should. They will,
Susy. Suddenly it will begin to happen, though at first
you'll hardly realise it. The main thing is not to worry.
Have faith in yourself. . .'

Faith. . . Susy thought of her brother's quotation,
and blessed her mother for using the word again. 'I'm
sure you're right, Mum. . .' she said softly.

'I am, dear, you'll see. Now, I wondered if you'd like to come down to the beach this afternoon when I take two of the children from the home?'

Susy didn't answer as her mother went on, 'It's Robin and Sandra today. I have a feeling my usual partner won't be able to make it, and I just wondered. . .'

'I don't think so, Mum; I. . .' The phone buzzed and her mother answered.

'You can't. I am sorry. No, not to worry. . .' She replaced the receiver, giving a sigh. 'As I thought, her little girl's sickening for something so I'll ring around. . .'

A pang of conscience hit Susy when she saw her mother's anxious frown. 'OK, dear, don't bother, I'll come.'

In the car on the way to the orphanage, Dorothy told Susy about her two young charges.

'Robin Masters is six, a rather introspective little boy, brightly intelligent, but for a child so young he tends to be a bit withdrawn from everyone except Sandra, the little girl he seems to have taken to. Anyhow, he's a delightful child with a mop of copper curls, large blue eyes, rosy cheeks, freckles and a smile that's extremely polite on the one hand, but I'm sure given half a chance could be full of devilment on the other. He's been at the home only a few months since his teenage mother died. She never came to see him before that, I'm told, or very rarely. Robin's one of those sad cases where his mother took up with a drug-taking crowd, and when she became pregnant tried to abort unsuccessfully; consequently Robin's little feet were deformed at birth. He has spent most of his life in hospital having had several ops, but so far there seems to have been no complete recovery. When the girl died from an overdose, the authorities, thinking he might be fretting for his mother — any mother —

decided to make a complete change and have him over here to live at the home and make a fresh start. Hopefully he'll settle down eventually, and one day may be adopted or fostered.'

'Poor little boy. And the girl?'

'Well, Sandra's rather different. She was left on the doorstep of a mainland hospital and no one ever claimed her. The same age as Robin and yet already she seems to be developing a mothering instinct for him. A very sensible child, a sort of no-nonsense approach, a true survivor. Her plain little face is quite elfin-like with huge blue eyes and a little pointed chin, and, of course, a sweet smile that few can resist. Robin responds to her well, which is something. At times, I'm told, they sit talking to each other in their wheelchairs like two little old adults. Sandra, you see, has MS and is likely to be disabled for the rest of her life.'

Susy gave a huge sigh as they turned in to a flower-edged drive. 'Why is the world so harsh. . .?'

'Heaven knows, darling. We can only do what we can to help.'

The safe beach was a broad gold crescent of fine silvery sand with coves and small rock pools ideal for children. After manoeuvring their two charges from the car and into the wheelchairs, Susy and Dorothy pushed them down the ramp cut into the cliff recently by an understanding council, which led them straight on to the hard-packed sand underfoot.

Introductions having already been made, Robin was silent. Sandra was chattering nineteen to the dozen to Dorothy, while Susy glanced down at the back of the small boy's curls glinting in the sun, small ears flat and pink against the well-shaped head, sturdy little shoulders encased in a red cotton T-shirt, and the soft, bare 'baby' neck at the back, just asking to be kissed, tugging at her heart. 'So how old are you, Robin?' Susy asked him brightly.

He turned his head to look up at her, the round eyes too old for his face. 'I'm six years and six months,' he piped up firmly.

'I'm the same,' called Sandra, not to be outdone.

Robin gave her a disdainful glance. 'Yes, but my birthday's on Christmas Day; yours isn't, it's two days after that.'

Dorothy and Susy exchanged grins that the boy had said so much, now even his young face looked more animated than usual.

'Right, OK, great! Aunty Dorothy and I now know both your birthdays and that's very important. Next, which game would you like to play first?'

Surprisingly Robin answered straight off. 'Can we play with the ball, please?'

Sandra squeaked with delight, clapping her hands with glee, quite obviously Robin's sidekick. 'Please, Susy, please, Aunty Dorothy, may we?'

Rounders was a great success, with Susy charging up and down the beach to retrieve the ball while the children took it in turns to bat from their chairs, nearly in hysterics with excitement when they scored a hit as close to the water's edge as possible, with Robin yelling, 'Go on, Susy, run! Good old Susy, throw it back to me!'

Eventually even the children tired and wanted some less energetic entertainment, and Dorothy flopped down on to a suitable rock, while Susy fetched handfuls of sea-shells for them to sort out with a points system awarded by Dorothy for a pearl, white, speckled or black one. 'Now,' she announced finally, 'as a souvenir to take home, I'd like a large piece of seaweed, please, for each of you.'

Susy obliged and honour was satisfied, almost. . .

'Mine's the biggest. . .'

'No, mine is!'

'She's wrong, isn't she, Susy? I won, didn't I?'

'I'd say you both won,' Susy laughed, opening a packet of chocolate and handing it round. 'I should think you need your tea now.'

As they went across the sand, Robin looked up anxiously at Susy. 'We're not going back to the home yet, are we?'

'Of course not, poppet; I happen to know Aunty Dorothy has something special for tea today!'

The kitchen at Rosebriar Cottage rang with the children's chatter and happy laughter, and when it was time for them to leave Robin seemed quite ready once he knew there was a possibility of their going out again soon. Sandra was contented, too, with her stoic attitude to everything that came her way.

After returning the children, Dorothy drove home to St John's Bay and smiled at her daughter. 'Thanks, darling—hope it wasn't too much for you?'

'No, I enjoyed it, Mum. As a matter of fact I half promised Robin I'd take him out again tomorrow, but I don't know if you were planning anything and perhaps can't manage Sandra?'

'Don't worry about that. If one of us wishes to take a child out singly as an extra treat, that's fine with the staff at the home; they'll make sure Sandra has a little outing of some sort while Robin's away. They're such a nice crowd. Matron's married, you know, with three teenagers of her own.'

'Yes, she seems a lovely motherly lady,' Susy answered vaguely, but her thoughts were partly on Robin as she said, 'You know, I think Robin could gradually become a happier, more integrated child. I think you can see the signs, and yet I can sense what you mean about the quiet loneliness of him. Still, he did join in this afternoon.'

'Thank goodness,' her mother rejoined, 'Matron looked quite bucked up when she saw him, I thought.'

That evening Ian Frenais listened with interest to

their account of the day, saying, as Susy removed the dishes from the dining table, 'As a matter of fact I seem to have had quite a good day myself!'

'What happened, dear?' Dorothy called, stacking the dishwasher in the kitchen.

'Well, at long last all the new equipment's installed at the peds unit! I can hardly believe it; it looks really splendid.' As Dorothy brought the coffee in, he said casually to his daughter, 'Why don't you pop in and have a look some time, Susy? There'll be someone there even if I'm not.'

Susy felt the old familiar cringing and shied nervously from the suggestion. 'Thanks, Dad, but there's little point really. . .'

Her parents' eyes met, but her father said with a smile, 'Just a passing thought, my dear.'

Three days later, Susy was driving her mother's VW Golf into St Helier for some extra preserving jars for the gooseberry jam which could not be obtained in the village. She had always enjoyed driving and had been the proud possessor of her own car in Belfast, but Patrick had worried about the dangerous aspects that constantly arose, particularly with parked cars, and she had sold it. Now, she revelled in the heady exhilaration of rushing through the country lanes between high lush hedges with the sun-roof pushed back. For a while there was nothing on her mind except the shush of the scented summer breeze and the contented hum of the car's engine. Too soon, holiday traffic began to appear as they converged upon St Helier which was already becoming crowded with visitors of every nationality, it seemed, and concentration was necessary.

Parking was no problem, and she managed to track down her mother's purchases and suntan lotion for herself, while trying not to notice the many holidaying couples both young and old drifting along happily hand in hand. She couldn't bear it, and abruptly turned into the nearest shop, which happened to be a florist, and bought her mother a huge bunch of flowers despite the fact that the house and garden were full of them.

Back in the car park which was by now very packed indeed, Susy stared nonplussed along the rows of coloured vehicles, doubting she'd ever spot her mother's.

'Why don't you whistle, and it'll come to you?' a deep male voice called.

Ross Beaumaris was striding leisurely towards her, a friendly grin on his face and looking very much younger in jeans, a navy cotton polo shirt, yet, with the professional status of his job, Susy knew he had to be around thirty-five. Thank heaven she was dressed more reasonably in a sundress rather than shorts this time. 'Hi!' she smiled. 'I might have to resort to your suggestion yet! The place was empty half an hour ago.'

He grinned, strong good teeth flashing, lean chiselled features very self-assured, a man completely at ease with himself and the rest of the world, with no doubt bags of charm to spare for absent-minded females. The thought made her pull back her shoulders and lift her chin, making her sun-flecked hair skim her shoulders, her compelling brown velvety eyes taking on a brighter lustre as she grinned back when he said, 'Well, well, seeing that we've already been introduced over the gooseberries, why don't we go and have a coffee? By that time your car might reveal itself to you!'

'Right, why not?' she countered, feeling slightly light-headed.

'Great! Come on, then,' he said decisively. 'I know a continental café in a little side-street, complete with cobbles underfoot and traffic banned.'

'Hey, that could be the beginnings of a pop song and you could make your fortune!'

'Susy, you have some wonderful ideas!'

They sat beneath white and green striped umbrella

tables, where every other shop was a café or boutique, baskets of flowers cascaded everywhere and French accordion music floated through an open doorway. When Ross had ordered, she was conscious of him studying her face, neck and bare tanned shoulders, saying with laughter in his voice, 'I hope you don't mind me calling you by your first name?'

'No. I'll call you Ross from now on, then we're quits!'

'That's a good start anyway!'

'I've heard Dad speak of you often. It sort of comes naturally, I suppose.'

'It's definitely my lucky day, that's for sure!'

Little bubbles of mirth welled up inside her. 'Don't push it, though, Ross; I'm not a bit interesting, you know!'

'Now that I do not believe. In fact, I'll go so far as saying I *will* not believe!'

She sipped her coffee, and it was as if she'd had a sudden replay in her head of the nonsense they'd bandied between them. What on earth was she thinking? She felt a traitor to Patrick's memory, and this led to a sudden sense of withdrawal from this laughing man. Already her lowering spirits were taking her down far enough to see that he was probably laughing *at* her, not *with* her. She couldn't possibly be anything like the young sophisticates with whom he no doubt mixed. She had almost forgotten what it was like to indulge in crazy talk and flirtatious back-chat the way it used to be before Patrick.

'Susy, are you OK?' She realised Ross was loooking at her oddly. 'Not something I said, I hope?' His eyes were concerned. 'You look quite pale suddenly.'

She gave a wan smile. 'Oh, no, I'm OK, thanks. I think I'd better be going, though.'

'But why? You've hardly finished your coffee.' His mouth lifted at the corners. 'You can't do that to me!'

All the joky repartee had gone from her as she said quietly, 'Sorry. Ross, my mother needs these jars.'

She knew she sounded fatuous, but now it no longer mattered. All she wanted was to escape those astute laughing eyes, retreat back into her silent world where she could recall Patrick and the way they were. She realised Ross was speaking to her. She brushed a hand across her forehead as if fending off a headache. 'Sorry, Ross, I didn't quite catch what you said then.'

'Nothing important; I just wondered if, while you're in town, you might like to come over to the General with me to see the new unit?'

'Well,' she replied, her voice sounding a long way off, 'I don't think I have the time really.'

CHAPTER TWO

THE surprising invitation from Ross had stopped Susy in her tracks, the unexpectedness of it suddenly clearing her mind of its downbeat trend. Hadn't her father suggested she visit the unit, which she had rejected earlier because he understood all the circumstances? Whereas now she was sure Ross had no idea of the full story — simply because she had asked her parents not to put it around — and so in a perverse sort of way she could accept the offer as well as see the new wing.

Her father was ever hopeful that she would change her mind, but wih Ross Beaumaris there was no such pressure. As far as he was concerned, she was an orthopaedic nursing sister home on leave, and it would seem to be the most natural thing in the world for her to be deeply interested in her own subject. And wasn't she still? a small inner voice whispered.

'On second thoughts——' she gave him a delectable smile '—if you don't mind my having them, may I change my mind?'

Ross wondered, not for the first time, what lay behind this girl's attractions, most of which seemed to alternate between sunlight and shadow that emanated from deep within her, as if an all-pervading unhappiness was holding back her natural spontaneity and zest for life. He returned her smile with an enthusiastic nod. 'Isn't that always the female prerogative? There's no need to ask; I'll be only too delighted to show you over. How about another coffee, if you'd like it, and then we'll go?'

In the car park, as Ross had predicted, Susy found her car with no trouble, and he helped her pack the

parcels and flowers in before she was ready to set off.
She followed his grey BMW out towards Gloucester
Road on the outskirts of town, and in minutes they
were turning into the sprawling, modern red-bricked
hospital that she knew of old. After parking, they went
to the new unit where a few remaining workmen were
still dealing with finishing touches both outside and in.

'Welcome!' Ross said breezily, holding the door
open for her.

With a slight tension at her temples, Susy stepped
inside the as yet unmanned reception area. Ross was
already explaining the layout, and while listening with
half an ear she caught a glimpse through the connecting
door of the main building at the height of the midday
bustle. A rush of emotion swamped her, a mixture of
love for her job and the old familiar fear stemming
from lack of confidence in her own capabilities. Many
a sleepless night had still not provided her with the
answer, and until that time came she could not alter
her decision to give up nursing even though her medical
advisers in Belfast had tried hard to convince her she
would feel otherwise in the fullness of time. But she
knew that until — if ever — her own instincts and belief
in herself were right it would be impossible to make a
fresh start anywhere, let alone here, where she'd
started her training. The conclusion had to be hers
alone. . . Ross's deep, pleasant voice filtered back into
her thoughts.

'In here we have a communal and TV room for some
of the older teenagers and ——'

'Susy! Susy Frenais!'

A female voice broke in on Ross's commentary, a
pair of plump arms were flung around Susy, and there
was one of her best friends from training days. 'Julia!
This is terrific! How are you?' The two gazed at each
other in sheer pleasure and amazement.

Julia Fornet, looking the large, happy girl she'd

always been, glanced quickly at Ross. 'Forgive this interruption, Doctor, but it must be three years since we last met. Initially we did some of our training together here!'

Ross smiled. 'Don't mind me,' he said amiably. 'You two must have quite a lot of news to catch up on!'

'We certainly have, Ross,' Susy enthused, eyes shining. 'What about coming over to my place, Julia? I'll give you a call, shall I?'

Julia clapped her on the shoulder with a big grin. 'Smashing! Don't forget! I'd better let you get on with the conducted tour now. See you soon!'

Ross didn't appear at all put out as they carried on walking into the small, very modern, very well-equipped wards, an added bonus for children with long-stay problems, and how very un-hospital-like it looked. 'It's great, Ross. I can see why Dad's so thrilled.'

'I know. We're all a bit that way.'

She still felt slightly on edge. 'Hope you didn't mind that interruption just now; it's really been ages.'

He gave a wide smile. 'Susy, stop worrying about it! My life is made up of interruptions and surprises!' His shrewd eyes held hers briefly. 'Is there anything else worrying you? That's far more important; remember you're on holiday!'

Again he noticed a shadow pass across her face, as if what he'd said had touched upon a raw nerve-ending. He could have kicked himself for being so outspoken. It was a habit that often got him into hot water, not least with the wife he'd been only too glad to divorce. Although he thought of her rarely these days, it reminded him that the girl at his side, or any other attractive woman for that matter, would have to be one in a million before he ever took the plunge again!

Susy had taken his last remark seriously, it seemed. 'Surely we all worry, even on holiday, Ross?'

'I grant you that, but everything in perspective, eh?' he admonished jovially.

'Well. . .yes.'

'We'll forget our troubles for the moment, anyway. Tell me that you're glad you came here after all?'

'Definitely. I've thoroughly enjoyed it.'

'It's not over yet,' he said, as they went through more of the well-proportioned rooms. He pointed to tiers of racks around one of them. 'As you can see, this is the equipment-room, well-stocked with new splints, crutches, slings and frames. All this and much more besides. Through that archway are the larger medical aids.'

'Superb,' Susy agreed. 'I can remember all too often having to run around from one ward to another when we were suddenly short of a Robert Jones brace or a Thomas's bed knee splint.'

'Yes, in certain places it still goes on, unfortunately. But here we hope it will be very different with only four to a ward. Each ward, incidentally, will have its own small dressings-room, as well as bathrooms, an exercise area like a mini gym, and, of course, a splendid kitchen. Oh, yes, and this super playroom is for young patients once they can start getting around on their own, and of course there's a schoolroom, too.'

Susy was very impressed at the way Ross Beaumaris's face lit up at the prospect of putting the new unit into action. A love of children shone through his every word. 'How many of these special wards have you?' she asked.

'Six at present, which will have to last a few years, I'm afraid, but we're ever hopeful that one day more might be added; there's enough land for it. One of our rich philanthropists had the foresight to buy it a hundred or so years ago; it's worth a small fortune now.'

'That worthy gentleman would be proud of this

complex. I just love the airiness of it all; the sliding doors too almost bring the gardens inside.'

'Yes, and note the animals and children's TV favourites specially patterned on the glass in colour, so that in their excitement to get outside they don't forget the glass doors are there. They are heavily reinforced ones, but we can't take any chances.' He added, 'I'm sure you've heard of that dauntless lady, Dame Agnes Hunt?'

'Oh, yes, she worked for crippled children all her life, being one herself since childhood.'

'Right. Together with Sir Robert Jones, of equal fame, they did a great deal to advance orthopaedic work to what it is today. The Shropshire Orthopaedic Hospital originated from the ramshackle old buildings of the Baschurch Home opened by Dame Agnes at the turn of the century.'

'Yes, and we're still practising her theory that treatment should always be based on rest, fresh air, surgery and happiness.'

'Indeed.' He glanced suddenly at his wristwatch. 'Drat! How time flies. I'm afraid I must go, Susy, and I've already kept you longer than I intended. Did you want to see Ian while you're here? I could soon make contact.'

'No, thanks, it's not necessary. You've been an excellent guide and that makes all the difference!'

He looked pleased; the girl knew her stuff when it came to the nuts and bolts of her subject, even more so when she forgot her hang-ups. 'Nice of you to say so! Come in any time.'

They went out to the car park, still talking about the unit. He opened her car door, smiling briefly, and again she detected that faint suggestion of laughter in his gaze, with perhaps a dash of male chauvinism, rather than patronage, as she had at first thought. Being in such close proximity, she noticed a small scar along the edge of his chin, an abstracted observation, but still one that seemed to make him just as vulnerable as everyone else. Sliding into the driving seat, she thanked him again, switched on the ignition and opened the window. 'I've really appreciated the tour. I do wish you luck with keeping the project afloat financially if I don't see you again.'

One smooth dark eyebrow lifted very slightly. 'I do hope that won't be the case,' he said, with irresistible charm. 'Besides, as for keeping afloat, it's people like your splendid mother who'll make sure that it does!' He noticed a delightful crinkling of her pert nose as the car began to move, when she called with a grin,

'That reminds me, it may not be, if Mum doesn't soon get her new jam-jars. Bye, now!'

At Rosebriar Cottage, her mother immediately made tea and they both sat at the kitchen table while Dorothy waited eagerly to hear about the morning once Susy told her where she had been. 'Well, that's terrific, dear! What did you think of all the wonderful labour-saving gadgetry? It has to be one of *the* ortho centres in the country!'

'Quite definitely. With everybody's enthusiasm, how can it possibly fail? I've never yet seen anything like it.' All Susy's impressions poured out, much to her mother's delight and relief, and she went on, 'I nearly forgot, Mum, we ran slap into Julia Fornet — you remember her?'

'Yes, of course! One of your old training friends!'

'It was sheer coincidence. I'm going to call her some time and we'll get together for a good natter. Do you know, I can't think if she ever heard that Patrick and I were engaged, or about our meeting? She and John have been abroad so much and are only just back, so it wouldn't be surprising. Then latterly I hadn't written. Still, we'll make up for it!' She jumped up suddenly, finishing her tea with a gulp. 'Sorry, Mum, I've just seen the time. I want to take Robin out again this afternoon; I don't want to let him down. Tell you more tonight.'

On the beach the warm but exhilarating fresh air fanned her face as she pushed Robin's wheelchair along while looking for a rock as a makeshift seat, preferably one that didn't argue with the contours of her own. Soon the joyful rush of the sea as it swirled around smaller rocks soothed away any slight tendency Susy had had to a headache earlier while with Ross. There had been so much to absorb, and he was. . . She cut off the thought abruptly, pulling her mind back to Robin, who had already asked several quite tricky questions and was no doubt lining up a few hundred more. At the moment he seemed to want to know all about her life from Day One. When it came to her age, she said flippantly, 'Robin, you don't really want to know?' She laughed, knowing that to a child of six even seventeen was knocking on a bit.

His voice was perky as he looked round at her with a cheeky grin which was becoming more prominent by the minute. 'Yes, I do, Susy. Sandra and I had guessing games the other night at teatime.'

'Oh, yes, and who won?'

'I did because I told her that we didn't really know and I must find out from you. Sandra said yes, I was right.'

Good old Sandra, Susy thought with a grin. That certainly follows; girls were ever practical no matter what age they were! 'Well,' she said, 'if I tell you twenty-five, you may not want me to take you out again!'

There was a brief pause, then the child said with serious consideration, 'I don't mind, I s'pose. At least you're still pretty and you can run.'

Susy decided to come clean and tell him the whole

dreadful truth. 'Well, on my next birthday I'll be. . .
How old?' She might as well have him make capital
out of this discussion if the young quiz-master's brain
was working along those lines.

'Twenty-six!' came back the reply, quick as a flash.
He did a swift calculation on his fingers. 'When you're
twenty-seven, Susy, will you still be able to take me
out then?'

A gale of laughter erupted from her. 'I should hope
so, darling! Come on now, let's see what sort of fruit
you'd like this afternoon. There's peaches, apples,
bananas. . .?'

'No, thanks, Susy, I wouldn't like any of those.'

'But you told me you loved fruit!'

A great sneeze suddenly exploded from him, then
another and they both laughed as he scrambled in his
pockets for a clean tissue. 'Sandra says she's got a
cold,' he said, 'and she's given it to me.'

'I shouldn't think so; it might be hay fever.'

'What's that?'

'Well, it's pollen dust from the flowers and grasses
that get into your nostrils and tickle.'

That struck him as hilarious, and when he'd stopped
laughing he said happily, 'I like you, Susy. Will you
always take me out?'

'Whenever I can, Robin, of course I will.'

He was silent when it was time to go back to the car,
and even once at the home he'd developed an air of
withdrawal, as if in some way she had let him down by
returning him.

That night before sleeping, the child's face troubled
her. It was the air of isolation which he seemed to
project so poignantly from time to time. Just like her
own, and in a strange sort of way he knew it too, and
she wanted to comfort him, rather as she needed
comfort herself, oh, so desperately.

Later that week Susy invited Julia and her husband

John to dinner. Her parents were at a bridge party and she enjoyed planning and cooking the food on her own. The table was set and finishing touches put to the meal when the phone rang. To her surprise it was Ross.

'Hi, Susy. I know this is short notice, but what about having dinner with me tonight?' The laughter in his voice brought a smile to her face.

'Well, I'm awfully sorry, Ross, but. . .'

He broke in with mock-despair, 'Susy, you've hurt me deeply! Does this mean that after all you didn't like my conducted tour?'

'Not a bit of it,' she laughed, 'but Julia and her husband are coming to dinner tonight. Why don't you join us?' she said impulsively, the words slipped out before she could stop them. Wasn't asking him to make up a foursome rather pushy?

But his reply sounded easygoing enough. 'That's a very handsome offer. I'm not quite sure if I can get away early enough without spoiling all your arrangements, but I'll certainly try, if that's OK?'

'Sure! Don't feel pressured; I'll save yours just in case!'

'See you around eight, then, or as near as possible.'

She went upstairs to change, wondering if that conversation had actually taken place. Her moment of panic had subsided; after all, he was a friend of the family, and it would be quite a good idea if Ross could join them. At least it would be company for John while she and Julia exchanged news.

In the event Julia and John had so much to tell of their time abroad that they were still enjoying pre-dinner drinks when there was a ring at the front door.

'That must be Ross,' Susy said quickly, noticing the look of mild surprise on Julia's face. 'We were going out to dinner to talk shop,' she improvised, not quite knowing why, 'but I thought this would be even nicer!'

She hurried to the door and opened it. 'Hi, Ross!'

He was framed in the doorway, smiling, looking as immaculate in a silver-grey lounge suit as she would have imagined. He handed her a bottle of wine. 'Hello, Susy. I wasn't sure about this, but it might add to the stocks!'

'Thanks so much, Ross. Come out to the patio; we haven't even started dinner yet!'

Eventually they got round to eating and had coffee back on the patio while John regaled them with hospital talk of overseas establishments.

'What did you think of the Egyptian hospitals, John?' Ross asked, seated in a cane chair, one elbow nonchalantly looped over the back of it.

John's round, bespectacled face grinned. 'My dear old Ross, it would take me all night! Suffice it to say, though, they have some extremely good doctors out there. I've nothing but praise for them, but quite honestly they're fighting a losing battle both day and night.'

While the men talked, the two girls removed the debris from the dining-room table. 'We're not going to get our tête-à-tête now, Susy. Shall we meet in that little place we used to?'

The telephone interrupted them, Susy answered, then called, 'It's for you, Ross!'

He made a grimace, and, answering the phone, said briskly, 'Right, yes, I'll be there, I'll come immediately.'

He rejoined the others. 'Sorry about this; I have to go. It may be minutes, it may be longer. Sorry, Susy.'

'Don't worry. Come back if you can: we'll be talking for hours yet, I should think!'

When he'd gone, Julia said with a laugh, 'Poor old Ross; not one of us asked if he had far to go!'

'Why should *he* be any different, darling?' John said

reasonably. 'How often do you ask me where I'm going when I get a call out at, say, three in the morning?'

Susy giggled. 'Tell me what she does say, John?'

'Well, Susy, seeing that you're one of Julia's best friends and you won't hold it against her, I will! Her comments are always the same,' he went on. '"Oh, for God's sake, John, must you take the whole of the duvet with you?" And that, I might add, is mumbled in some near-incomprehensible jargon I've come to recognise as, I love you, darling, but I'm glad it's not me. Goodnight!'

Julia hooted with laughter. 'The truth at last! I didn't know I said anything like that, John. You're making it up!'

Listening to her friends' banter, although Susy had enjoyed the evening immensely, her spirits were beginning to deflate. Maybe it was the loving ding-dong going on between John and Julia, the way it might have been with Patrick and herself, the teasing and the ribbing, yet beneath it all the sureness of a love like an invincible scaffolding supporting their three-year-old marriage against all odds, and still no doubt strengthening.

She stood up suddenly, serving more coffee as John said reluctantly, 'Well, Susy, love, much as we hate to do it, I'm afraid we have to leave. I have an early start tomorrow and——' he chucked his wife playfully under the chin '—I know that Sister Fornet here has!'

Julia groaned. 'With two short on Medical, we're all general dogsbodies at the moment. I don't know why we carry on nursing, Susy. Do you ever think of opting out?'

Susy gulped. There had been little time to talk of future plans to Julia. She said quickly, 'Well, a lot of things have happened in the last couple of years, Julia; I must say I have actually considered it quite seriously, though.'

A small frown crossed Julia's face. 'Oh I didn't
know,' she said. 'Look. . .' John stood up, taking her
arm. 'OK, John, I'm coming! Susy, I have a bit of time
to spare tomorrow afternoon. What about coming to
the hospital? Then we can look for that place we used
to go to, and have a talk, or stay in the canteen,
whichever.'

'Yes. About two o'clock all right for you?'

Amid laughter and thanks, John eventually managed
to haul Julia away. Susy waved them off, then auto-
matically began collecting up glasses, while her mind
was partly on talking to Julia next day, and partly on
Ross, wondering if he'd still make a sudden reappear-
ance that evening.

Just after midnight her parents returned, but there
was no word from Ross and, feeling a slight sense of
disappointment, she went to bed. Even talking over
specific hospital affairs with her friends had renewed
the old sense of 'belonging', though she hadn't realised
that until now. Also it came as something of a shock
when she remembered Julia asking if she'd ever
thought of giving up nursing. She had been unable to
answer positively, lately something seemed to hold her
back, yet she knew that actually working in hospital at
present with dedication and a clear mind was quite a
different thing from reflections of the past. At length
she felt drowsy, her last dream-like vision of Patrick
drifting across her mind, but it was Ross Beaumaris's
face that she saw most clearly.

Next morning, Susy rang the home to check that she
could collect Robin for a couple of hours, but was
surprised when Matron said, 'I'm sorry, Miss Frenais,
he has rather a bad cold — could be a flu germ perhaps,
we're not quite sure, but I've kept him in bed. Last
night he seemed to be having a little trouble with his
breathing. I called in our regular doctor. He prescribed

a mild antibiotic, and said to let him know how Robin is in a day or two.'

'I'm sorry to hear that, Matron. Could I come and see him?'

'Well, for your sake, my dear — your mother tells me you're at home convalescing — I don't think it's wise at this stage, but if you'd like to ring at the end of the week I'm sure he'll be OK by then.'

That afternoon Julia and Susy found the small café they used to go to near the hospital, but it had been updated partially to a modern ice-cream parlour where children constantly flowed in and out, and the two friends agreed it had lost the charm it once had. 'Still, the coffee's not bad,' Julia grinned. 'Tell you what, come back to the senior common-room at the hospital and we can get a reasonable tea there from four o'clock on.'

Susy panicked suddenly. The idea of being drawn back again amid the sort of people she was so used to, yet had a fear of, made her quake inside.

Julia hardly noticed her hesitation as she romped on, 'First, carry on telling me what's been happening? You got to the bit where you met this gorgeous guy who was in the Army, Susy. He had just been away on a course to get his commission, then he was stationed in Belfast where you met him at a dance!'

Susy took a deep breath; it was rather like preparing to jump into a bottomless pit. 'Well. . .' She looked up into her friend's grey eyes. 'Julia, this is in confidence. I don't find it easy to talk about, and I certainly don't want it spread around.'

Julia shook her head. 'Haven't we known each other long enough for you to take that for granted, Frenais?' she murmured, dropping back to the affectionate use of surnames as they had during their training, and now emerging in the form of positive reassurance.

'I'm know, I'm sorry, I shouldn't have said that.

Anyway, everything was wonderful with Patrick and me. We met each other's parents, got engaged, organised the wedding all in about six months. We were so happy, and with me working at the Belfast General we were able to see each other quite often. Yet I thought somehow it couldn't last. I just couldn't shake off the feeling. Then. . .' She kept her voice steady, retelling the event the way it was and '. . .Well, there was this car booby-trapped in the street. It exploded and he was killed.' Tears caught at her throat as the words faded but the picture remained.

Julia's hand covered hers. 'Oh, my God, Susy,' she whispered. 'I'm so sorry; I had no idea.'

Susy blew her nose, a smile breaking through as she watched another gang of little ice-cream marauders marching into the shop. 'Look, let's go back to the hospital and find that tea, shall we?' Her nervousness had suddenly left her. A small oasis of calm had taken its place, and she was honestly coming to believe that, thinking about Patrick, talking about him, it was as if he were helping her too.

CHAPTER THREE

THE senior common-room at the hospital was empty but for an untidy array of abandoned easy-chairs; nevertheless, it was large and comfortable, tastefully curtained and carpeted in dark green and rose, with a library corner in pine and a small TV room off the main area that did not disturb weary workers.

Julia and Susy collected tea-trays from an alcove bar at the entrance, carrying on their conversation. Julia still looking deeply concerned at what Susy had already told her.

'I just wish I'd known before,' Julia said worriedly as they sat down. 'Seeing that you'd had a breakdown and had been sent home and all the rest of it, Susy, at the very least I wouldn't have dreamed of descending on you last night for dinner.'

'Don't be crazy, Julia. I loved it. It's the first time in ages I began to feel normal.'

'Do you mean that?'

'Cross my heart, I do. Don't forget I'm convalescent now. If I don't make some real progress while I'm home, that's the time for the worrying to start.'

Julia poured the tea. 'But Susy, love, what's this about giving up work? You can't mean it surely?'

Susy's animation sudddenly left her face. 'I don't think I've the confidence to take on responsibility any more,' she said quietly. 'You know how it is yourself, Julia; there just has to be that unswerving belief inside that you're good at the job. Not to be swollen-headed about it, but to have the indefinable sense of knowing that you are a square peg in a square hole. And quite

honestly I haven't yet regained that feeling, and I can't
take any risks.'

'Have you talked to anyone else about this?'

'My parents, but no one else. For one thing I didn't
care to and, well, it seemed just as painful for me to
bring it out in the open as saying nothing at all, so I've
sort of brought the shutters down on it for a while.'

'Susy, you must talk about it. What you've told me
is obviously a step forward but somehow you have to
find your way back to your old self.'

Julia sensed Susy's sudden withdrawal by the look of
quiet desperation in her eyes, and said brightly, 'Hey,
tell me a little more about the children at the home;
we were sidetracked last night with your hospitality!'

Susy seemed to come back to life again as her lovely
eyes shone. 'Yes, well, it's Mum's doing really. Already
she has some of the disabled children under her wing,
and I stepped in to help, though with some
hesitation. . .'

'What do you have to do?'

Briefly, Susy explained the routine. 'The boy who
seems to have latched on to me is called Robin
Masters — he's a lovely little six-year-old, cute to look
at, has the devil in his eyes and silver in his tongue —
when he speaks, that is. Apart from that, he's basically
fretting for a mum and a proper home. A funny child —
he tells me all sorts of strange grown-up things; far *too*
sensible, if you know what I mean, I can't help taking
to him.'

Julia eyed her friend thoughtfully. 'Has he any other
friends at the home?'

'Yes, Sandra's his favourite, they're nearly insepar-
able, but I get the feeling he's reserved about the things
that mean a lot to him, the deep-seated need for love,
which may not be expressed in words, but breaks out
in other ways.'

'It could be that you are both doing each other a favour if he confides in you.'

Susy smiled. 'Well, I don't know if it's anything so profound as that, but I certainly enjoy his company, and having something specific to do.'

'Talking of things to do, how come Ross Beaumaris has his eyes on you?' Julia said suddenly, with her usual forthrightness.

Susy felt herself blush. 'Now, Julia, don't start getting up to your old matchmaking tricks again. Do you remember when we. . .?'

Amid laughter they immediately propelled each other back into their 'murky' past, about boyfriends who came and went, and how they used to talk endlessly to each other reporting on their current affairs and miseries, until they had both been transferred to different hospitals once qualified. 'Hell, those were the days. . .' Julia giggled.

'So how did you meet John?' Susy asked. 'He's so nice.'

'He joined the maternity unit here just after you left. He used to ask me to play badminton. Only because he was better at it than me—that's what I tell him, anyway! Then we just seemed to jell, and realised. . . we realised. . .' Julia searched hard for something to say that didn't sound too perfect to the heartbroken girl's ears '. . .well, that it was bigger than both of us!'

Fortunately both had the same zany sense of humour, and they dissolved into fresh spasms of laughter until the intercom burst into life. 'Sister Fornet! Will Sister Fornet of Primrose Ward please come to Reception? She's wanted on the telephone.'

'Hell's bells!' Julia glanced at the clock on the wall, and jumped up. 'I bet that's John; he thinks I'm back on duty. I must fly, love.' She gave Susy a big hug. 'Look, I'll give you a ring in a day or two and we'll get together again.'

Susy finished her tea, thinking she might try and see
her father. There were very few people left whom she
knew at the hospital now, apart from Julia, but, even
though some staff had wandered into the room for tea,
it still remained pleasant to feel part of a community
whether she knew them or not. It had been good
talking to Julia, just like the old days when they had
quite literally told each other everything. She supposed
it must have been while working in Belfast that she had
become slightly more reticent, in particular once she
was given a ward as a junior sister in her early days
there. Then when she'd met Patrick he'd been all she
needed when it came to advice, opinions, love.

'Well, well, well, if it isn't Susy!'

Ross Beaumaris had entered the room and stopped
in his tracks when he saw her. Even his attractive
white-coated companion looked her way as Ross said
warmly, 'Rebecca, come and meet Susy Frenais, Ian's
daughter. Susy, Rebecca Cohen.'

'Miss Frenais, how nice to meet you,' the husky
voice drawled. 'Home on holiday?'

The girl was beautiful in a voluptuous, darkly dramatic sort of way, and looked as if her claws were
emerging slightly. Susy gave her a wide smile. 'Miss
Cohen, hello! More home than holiday at the moment,
I think!'

The large, sensuous eyes swept over her. 'I know
what you mean, my dear. However——' she smiled up
at Ross '——I'll leave you in Ross's tender care now, but
don't be fooled by it!' She laughed, before crossing the
room to join colleagues.

Ross pulled up a chair for himself beside hers,
smiling at Rebecca's departing back. 'Take no notice
of Rebecca; the minute she sees another attractive
female she acquires all the qualities of a chameleon, or
worse. Are you here to visit Ian? Is there anything I
can do?'

'No, nothing, thanks.' She told him about her afternoon with Julia. 'It was great; she's only just left. I was toying with the idea of tracking Dad down, but I don't think I will now; time's getting on.'

'Ah, I've ruined the plan.'

'Not at all; there never was a plan. Actually I'm glad to see you; we were all wondering how you got on last night as you didn't come back.'

'Yes, sorry about that. I saw the child in question, and no sooner had I got back here than two youngsters on whom I'd operated during the week needed further attention. By the time I'd finished, it was far too late to go over to St John's Bay. I intended ringing you, anyway, once I got off duty this afternoon, to explain.'

'There's no need.'

'I really enjoyed the time I spent with you all; it was great having a get-together like that.'

They talked on for a while until she stood up to leave. 'I must get back now.'

Outside they walked past Reception together, and almost immediately Susy was once again overcome with the same old feeling of inadequacy at the business-like bustle going on all around her. She had stayed in the building longer than she'd intended and with Julia gone, and Ross smiling down at her with those quizzical eyes, she was floundering. All she wanted now was to get back home. It was as if, having put so much effort into the night before as well as this afternoon, her newly acquired rational thinking had suddenly been eroded, leaving her bereft of any positive reserves. This, she knew, was the sort of thing that nagged away at her subconscious whenever she contemplated returning to nursing. It both terrified and mortified her at the same time. How could she ever surmount this problem if she were to consider taking up her normal life again?

Outside the hospital Ross was talking about further deliveries of fitments to the paediatric unit that morning, as they went over to the car park. He seemed unaware of a certain vagueness about her while he talked, and she tried to pick up what he was saying.

'So you see, if you'd like to come again at any time to see more of the place, you're very welcome. Although, as you said to Rebecca, it's more home than holiday!'

She laughed. 'Take no notice, I was just being flippant. It's great to be here at home and wallow in the ordinariness of things!'

'Well, in that case, do you feel like wallowing in the ordinariness of dinner tonight somewhere? We'll probably talk shop, but who cares? I'm more than interested to hear about Belfast for a start!'

She began to cringe again. 'Oh, I don't think that anything I can tell you will be so very different from what you read in the news,' she said diffidently.

'I'm sure that's not true, Susy. Let's prove it, then, shall we? What about if I pick you up at seven tonight? I'll tell you my life's history, if you're coy about yours!'

She always finished up laughing with him. 'Well, if you put it that way, seven o'clock it is!'

That evening they drove along the coast road to La Rocque, and sat in the Floral Conservatory with a drink before going into the main restaurant for dinner. The air was cooler than of late, and Susy was glad she'd worn her white cotton jersey dress. It was just right for the change in the atmosphere; and more importantly she had been determined to start using her trousseau clothes, garments she had at first left at home and intended never to wear again.

She met Ross's eyes suddenly over the rim of his wine glass. So many questions seemed to be there, and she lowered her own gaze, almost bracing herself for what he was about to say.

'Susy, what is it that makes me think on the one hand you are very happy in the medical profession, yet on the other there's something that. . .' he pursed his firm lips, a small crease formed on his brow '. . .that's holding you back—or am I getting it wrong? I could be, of course; you females are all adept at putting up smoke-screens!'

The gold chain at her neck glinted softly in the light of the mellow table-lamp between them. She smiled at his speculations; they were not far wrong. 'Ross, with regard to that last remark I think you're just a tiny bit cynical about the opposite sex!'

'You're changing the subject, but never mind!' He smiled wryly. 'But you're right. Getting divorced is not exactly a bundle of fun.'

'I'm sorry.'

'Don't be. I'm not. It was the best day's work I ever did. . .eventually.' He glanced up as the waiter told them their table was ready. Once seated and having ordered, they enjoyed the excellent food, Ross not referring again to his divorce, but keeping her amused with medical anecdotes collected from his training days at Guy's, and from his specialist work for children at the John Radlett Hospital in Oxford.

'At the time,' he smiled, 'one takes all the jokes and laughs for granted, but it's strange how subsequent incidents over the years often nudge a joke back to life again that's still relevant to the present. Humour has far more value intrinsically than we realise.'

'Yes, I've found the same, particularly at my last hospital. Genuine laughter is a million times better than a whole lot of pill-popping.'

'I imagine in Belfast it's a lifesaver.'

'Absolutely. In Casualty it certainly taught me a great deal about the amazing fortitude of people, although it was only for a few weeks.'

'What about your own fortitude?'

The question caught her off balance. Her heart tumbled over. She had hardly realised the way the

conversation had gone, her saying things she hadn't
mentioned for ages. But she couldn't talk to Ross
about Patrick. She couldn't. It had been different with
Julia, but this man with those astute, compassionate
eyes that seemed to probe her mind would need to
know too much, something as yet she was quite unable
to handle. She studied the almond-pink tablecloth,
murmuring without raising her eyes. 'Heavens, no. . .'

His firm, lean hand covered hers across the table and
she was compelled to meet his gaze as he said quietly,
'Some weeks ago now, before you came home, your
father told me that you had broken off your engagement. He gave no further details, naturally, but he
seemed very concerned about you. Now you're home
for a rest, which means things have really got you
down, which is not surprising. You certainly must have
needed fortitude, and you have my admiration, Susy.
As for commiserations, I'll say very little. Quite often
these things are meant to happen.'

Silently she thanked her father for not saying too
much about the apparent 'broken' engagement, as she
had asked him. In a more literal sense it was true; the
engagement had been broken off, irrevocably and
forever. Yet it was sufficient to know that her father
understood how she would have shied away from a
different kind of sympathy. Ross did not seem, nevertheless, the type to ask leading questions, and she was
grateful. She gave a small sigh. 'It's quite amazing what
we can endure when put to the test. I mean, you
yourself, Ross, must have gone through all the anguish
of a failed dream.'

He nodded, a sad, rueful smile about his lips. 'It's
true. The trouble with my wife was that she never
really grew up. Her father's a wealthy banker, and
Miriam was his only child, his wife having died years
before. Everything Miriam wanted, she had. Even after
we were married, if I didn't pander to her every whim,

her father did. It was nepotism gone mad. I came to realise she was both incompetent and basically lazy, so much so that she utterly refused to have children. It was the bitterest disappointment in my life. I suppose she wasn't a bad girl at heart, just thoroughly ruined by an over-indulgent father who, in his loneliness, lavished all his affection and wealth on his offspring. Miriam was quite happy to continue living off her father's money for the rest of her life, but when we were together, and she started amusing herself with admirers who found their way to her bed, I opted out.'

'That's really tough, Ross. Where did you meet?'

'We both belonged to the Yacht Club here. I've always done a lot of sailing, and I think she usually turned up to decorate the place. One doesn't see these things at the time. I was besotted and she was something of a catch.'

'Do you ever see her?'

'From time to time, yes. She still lives in our house on the island here, which her father had bought for us when we married. We're quite civilised to each other these days. Occasionally we turn up at the same parties. I suppose one could say we're friends, certainly on the surface, and that's vastly different from the way it used to be. On the whole it's turned out to be a fairly civilised arrangement. But —' he laughed with a shrug '— there's one thing I shall avoid in future.'

'Yes?'

'Should I ever meet anyone else remotely like Miriam, with a rich doting father, I'll run a mile!'

She smiled, thinking what a tragic quirk of fate that he should marry someone who did not want children, when his whole life was given over to other people's.

'Odd, isn't it?' she murmured. 'The way we think we hold all the cards to play out our life as best we can, but it's rarely that way at all.'

'I know, and the more we try to manipulate things, the more complicated it becomes!'

She stared into space briefly, murmuring, 'Quite honestly, I don't know why we bother.'

A broad smile tilted his lips. 'I do, Susy, because it's meeting attractive but sensible girls like you that gives hope to us vulnerable males, and we all too quickly allow ourselves to become ensnared again in the net of marriage!'

'There you are!' She bubbled into laughter. 'I am right; I still say you're cynical, Ross!'

He grinned, getting to his feet, loose-limbed, casually elegant, and momentarily Susy wondered how anyone in love with him would have denied such a person a family life. 'Not guilty, ma'am!' he said flippantly, extending a hand to her. 'Shall we have coffee in the small sun-room over there?'

They sat in the pleasant area where cane furniture and flowers were arranged. Their conversation drifted to books, music, theatre, and a mutual interest in travel.

Susy sighed wistfully. 'I should just love to go on a world cruise that would take a couple of years; I can think of nothing more perfect!'

'Hmm.' He looked at her with one raised eyebrow. 'Which rather brings me to what I was about to say, only in reverse!'

'And that is?'

He tried his coffee, and thoughtfully replaced the cup, giving her an oblique smile. 'When are you thinking of returning to work, or is that something you don't want to worry about just now?'

She pursed her lips, avoiding his eyes. 'Well, I haven't allowed myself to think of it yet, I'm afraid, but sooner or later a decision has to be made.'

'I hear that you've been taking out some of the children from the home regularly.'

'Well, just one.'

'What's the name? I get to know most of them there.'

'Robin. . . Robin Masters. For the last couple of days he's been in bed with a flu virus of some kind, so I haven't seen him. I've telephoned, of course. Which reminds me, I must do so again; I'm longing to see the little chap once he's better.'

'You know, that must be the youngster with the copper curls and freckles.'

She laughed. 'You've described him exactly; there couldn't be another quite the same.'

'In that case, he is the one I saw last night.'

'Matron did tell me they'd called in a doctor; I had no idea who it might be. So you'll be keeping a watchful eye on him from now on?'

'Definitely; I'll be going in tomorrow.' He smiled, and again she noticed the small scar on his chin and wondered how it had happened. He met her eyes. 'Now, no more shop. I'd much rather talk about you. Why don't we have a drink first?'

As dusk smudged the sky with a slow explosion of pinks, rose and violet, Susy sat back to enjoy Ross's easy company a little longer. Mentally, she tried to keep him at arm's length, but gradually, with his almost imperceptible and gentle encouragement, she found herself talking of her hospital experiences in Casualty and the great strain under which they all worked. As she recounted recollections of terrible injuries wrought by bombs planted to kill and maim, her wide-set, soft brown eyes were luminous, her voice dropped almost to a whisper as she said simply, 'Whenever possible, staff are given extended leave to recover from the stresses and strains, but,' she went on, noticing that his eyes never left her face, 'the satisfaction of such a job is hard to improve upon.'

'I would have expected you to say that, Susy.'

Her face lit up as she smiled, giving a small shrug of her shoulders, her lovely eyes widening as if she'd been released from a trance. 'Well, that's enough from me for one night, Ross! I'm rather unstoppable at times when I talk about work. I think seeing Julia this afternoon unlocked a few doors that have been closed for some time!'

'You're too modest, Susy!' he said softly. 'Now, funnily enough, I heard from a good friend and colleague of mine this morning, an American of Italian extraction. I believe he was in Belfast some time ago with a group of his countrymen, and possibly may have been over there since, but I'm sure he'd be delighted to meet you. He and I worked together for a time in the States; he's done a lot for Third World disaster victims, children particularly. Great chap, becoming quite a name to be reckoned with by all accounts. However, he hopes to be spending a few days here shortly and this is just the sort of update of yours he'd be interested in.'

'No, Ross, I wouldn't think so.' The thought of talking to a stranger when it was linked with such deeper emotions had sent a tidal wave of fear through her. Already she had said more than she intended to Ross but in a way he was. . .different, she was surprised to admit.

Vaguely she felt the gentle pressure of Ross's hand upon her arm as if he sensed her thoughts, his voice low as he said, 'Susy, please don't feel anxious. You don't have to meet anyone you don't want to. You've obviously been through great traumas, but as a doctor, believe me, in my opinion the only solution for your peace of mind is to lay a few ghosts; face what——' He broke off suddenly, concern clouding his features. 'My dear, you've gone so pale again — are you feeling all right? I'm so sorry; I shouldn't have talked at such length to you. I do apologise. . . I——'

She shook her head, interrupting him, her colour slowly returning. 'Please, Ross, don't. It's my fault. Once my thoughts return to Belfast and. . .and all it entailed, I'm transported back and everything becomes so real again. . .' She fought to stave off the wave of panic that his words had brought on — the ghosts. Her brain added the words, 'graves'. . .'death'. . .her tormented mind letting her down for a moment. The memory of Patrick, so full of life and laughter, then the terrible news. And later the gentle words of dear Father O'Hara, who had christened her as a baby, and agreed to travel to Jersey to marry them. His soft, soothing brogue swum into her mind. 'Patrick and yourself found true love, Susy; that is far more than many have in a lifetime. Grieve by all means, my dear, shed your tears, hold him in your heart's shrine forever as you journey further along the road which God has mapped out for you. . .' The memory of his voice faded and she said quickly, 'Ross, forgive me for my lapse. Others have endured far worse. Of course I'll see your friend, particularly if it helps with the work he's devoting his life to.'

Ross's eyes were full of compassion. 'That's terrific of you, Susy, thank you,' he answered quietly. 'But only if you're up to it when the time comes.'

They had more coffee, Ross watching over her cautiously for any further sign of the effect his thoughtless conversation had engendered. They moved on then to discussing friends and relatives, about an uncle of Ross's who was a sheep farmer in New Zealand, and his son whom Ross had never met.

'What about your parents, Ross?'

He looked withdrawn suddenly. 'Unfortunately neither is alive now. Dad, who was a pretty good surgeon, died in his early forties, and my mother followed shortly after. It was a true love match between them. I was at the start of my own medical training at the time and hardly realised the awful tragedy of it. They had doted on me and I suppose I rather took everything for granted. But having since married myself, with the disaster that turned out to be, I realise now what a marvellous upbringing they gave me. Sadly, I had no brothers or sisters, but they were the sort of parents I always hoped to emulate myself.' He grinned wryly. 'I wasn't a spoilt brat, I hasten to add! To stand on my own two feet from a very early age was all they asked of me. Education-wise I couldn't have had better. They certainly didn't catch me and dig me out each time I made my mistakes!'

Susy smiled at the frank truthfulness on Ross's face, having already deduced that he was stubborn and probably at times downright pedantic about his opinions; now it seemed he was a man of iron will, too. 'Your parents sound very much like my own, Ross. We both have quite a lot to be thankful for, especially when thinking of children like Robin.'

'I couldn't agree more.' He leaned back in his chair, his tall, strong figure only just fitting into the upholstery frame, long legs crossed, broad shoulders resting back easily. He was giving her the whole of his attention, making her wonder again what was really going on behind those midnight-blue eyes that could crinkle at the corners with laughter, soften with sympathy, and occasionally gleam with gentle irony; so very attractive in every way. She had purposely allowed herself to assess him, and her finding him so personable, she realised, was the reason she felt more at ease when discussing with him topics that were hard to bring out into the open. 'I do hope you haven't found this evening too low-key, Ross,' she said suddenly, fingering an earring rather unnecessarily.

'Far from it,' he came back immediately. 'It's been a great evening. We needed to talk.'

CHAPTER FOUR

WHEN Susy and Ross left the restaurant that evening, stars were strewn across the sky in one of nature's more generous moods. Driving home with him, she felt more relaxed than she had for a very long time. Their conversation had shown that they had many interests in common, which was a good foundation for getting to know her parents' colleagues and friends.

They braked outside the house and Ross switched off the engine, leaving only the silence of the night surrounding them, and through the open windows they could hear wood pigeons cooing in the trees. Susy was suddenly very conscious of Ross at her side, and as she turned to speak to him she knew he had been looking at her with that questing gaze of his.

'Will you come in, Ross?'

'Thank you, Susy, but no.' His rich baritone fell softly into the quiet all around them. 'You need your rest after what happened this evening.' His dark, unfathomable eyes held hers. 'I do hope my thoughtless remarks about Belfast haven't prevented our going out again one evening?'

She smiled, the planes and contours of her face perfect in the shadows. 'Of course not; it was just one of those unexpected downturns that come and go with me at the moment. Still, things are getting better all the time.'

Her perfume assailed his nostrils as it had off and on all evening. He wanted to take her in his arms, try to understand exactly what sort of catastrophic unhappiness blunted her capacity to live as she should, while she was trying to cast off the Belfast experience and

become the attractive young woman eager for life and
love that she ought to be. He gave her a sardonic smile.
'You're very generous, Susy, but I'd never forgive
myself if each time we went out you experienced
something similar! I'm worried about you, you know.
Is there anything deep down that you want to talk
about? I mean some other time? You know I'll help if
I can.'

She touched his hand. 'Thank you, Ross, I do
appreciate your concern, but. . .but I'm OK. Coming
out like this this evening has been great.'

'Well, I'm relieved you feel that way.' His hand
brushed her shoulder. 'You know, it's good to see you
smiling; you must do that more often too!'

He got out of the car and opened her door, taking
her hand as she placed a slim, sandalled foot on to the
gravelled drive, high heels bringing her up only to his
shoulder. His hand tightened upon hers as she steadied
her balance on the stone chips underfoot, laughing at
her own apparent clumsiness. 'Oh, dear, why do we
girls wear such crazy shoes?'

He laughed. 'Because you are so charmingly feminine, Susy, that's why!'

It was a diplomatic reply. Had he but known, it was
nothing to do with her high heels or the gravel, but the
touch of his hand grasping hers so firmly, his cool skin
against hers. And, with a sense of shock, the sudden
umistakable telltale tingle that ran through her fingers
caught her unawares. Rather breathlessly, she thanked
him again. 'Goodnight, Ross, I've so enjoyed this
evening.' She fumbled for her latchkey as she walked
to the front door, glancing over her shoulder at him,
saying, 'You will let me know about Robin if possible,
won't you?'

He was back in the car, smiling from the open
window as he switched on the ignition. 'You can count
on it! Bye, now!'

With a softly expensive zoom the car disappeared out of the drive, and as Susy let herself into the house and went upstairs quietly, hoping not to disturb her parents, her brain was busy with the fact that instead of bemoaning that her life meant very little to her any more she was focusing on such a minor thing as two people's hands touching, and why something akin to an electrical current could shoot through her veins at the contact. The only time this had ever happened to her before was when she had been sixteen and still at school. She had had a crush on one of the English teachers at least ten years older than herself. When he'd told her he was engaged to be married, she had cried and cried for months afterwards. After confiding in her best friend, she had been told by her friend that this indicated a deep and inexplicable physical attraction between two people, having read this in one of her mother's magazines. It could also be true love or a passing fancy.

Susy had remembered the occasion almost as part of her early experience of relationships, but had certainly never experienced it with the same ferocity until now. The impact Patrick had had upon her senses had been more restrained. Theirs had been a slow burgeoning of love from friendship, nothing that made her feel the mere proximity of someone else was like a lighted fuse running inexorably towards a stick of dynamite.

Once in bed she suffered pangs of guilt about her inner thoughts. After all, her and Patrick's love had been going to be the enduring kind, the sort to make a marriage last. Yet now it was quite a revelation to discover that the other knowledge tucked away deep in the recesses of her mind was not quite as far away as she'd thought. Why Ross Beaumaris? It had to be just a passing phase after a pleasant evening. The whole thing had rather unsettled her, and with so many other problems on her mind she was not looking for further complications.

Her final thought before falling asleep that night was that she had truly loved Patrick, and that any emotional feelings for Ross Beaumaris were wasted. Had she not learned already that he was cynical about women, his career was everything, and he was not averse to glamorous medics like Rebecca Cohen trailing around at his side?

It was early next morning when her sleep was disturbed by the ringing of her bedside telephone. Drowsily she stretched out a hand and picked up the receiver. 'Hello, Susy Frenais. . .'

The deep voice made her sit up sharply. 'Susy! Ross Beaumaris. Sorry if I've disturbed your beauty sleep but I did promise to let you know how Robin was.'

What, at this hour of the morning? She pushed her hair out of her eyes. 'Hi, Ross; yes, go ahead.'

'Well, the news isn't too good, I'm afraid. We've confirmed that the little chap has contracted some kind of virus. He has a throat infection which could also reach the lungs. However, I'm not taking any chances and I'm having him brought in here to the peds unit for a day or two just to keep an eye on him.'

'Is he running a temp?'

'At the moment, yes. The ambulance is bringing him in now so I can let you know more details later. Your father will be here on his way to the consulting-rooms in an hour or so; we'll have a further discussion on the child then.'

'Right, thanks so much for letting me know, Ross. Not much chance of seeing him in a day or two, then?'

'Hopefully, yes. But at present I think we'll just let the drugs take over.'

'OK, thanks again. . .' She hesitated, suddenly running out of words. Her traitorous mind, now fully alert, was reminding her of the chemistry between them the

night before, and it prevented her from thinking of
anything sensible to say. Fortunately Ross hadn't been
struck in the same way.

'I hope you're not too tired after all the talking we
did last night?'

'Oh, no.' She laughed. 'I'm sure it did me a lot of
good, anyway.'

'That's terrific! Well, I must go. I'll keep in touch;
bye, now.'

Slowly she replaced the receiver, the quiet, com-
manding voice still resounding in her ear, his smiling
face in her mind's eye as if he were in the room with
her. She drew up her knees, elbows resting on them, a
far-away look in her eyes as she tried to dissociate him
from the other, more pressing problems bothering her,
but found it near impossible to do so.

For the rest of the day Susy helped her mother in the
garden, and gradually her thoughts cleared and the
main person on her mind was Robin. At lunchtime her
father came home to tell her what he could about the
child. 'These children are quite susceptible to such
viruses, Susy, as you know. Ross has done the right
thing, and now it's just a question of waiting to see
what happens in the next twenty-four hours.'

When he had gone Susy still could not shake off her
feeling of anxiety for the child. She knew he was in
good hands, but could not forget the look of deep
loneliness in his eyes when he had talked to her on the
day they were last out together. Even at six years old
he seemed to have a world of isolation in that
expression, yet always there was a hint of defensive-
ness, as if he intended fending off any direct sympathy;
he didn't need it; it was something he alone could
handle.

But, lying in the hospital as he was now, in a fever
and his little mind no doubt troubled with a series of
impressions both shadowy and frightening as he drifted

in and out of sleep, resistance would be difficult to summon up.

By eight o'clock that evening, when her father had not arrived home, and there had been no telephone calls from either him or Ross, Susy's hand was on the receiver to contact the hospital. She could wait no longer to hear how the child was, when to her great relief it rang. Eagerly she picked it up. 'Susy Frenais. . .'

'Ah, Susy. . .' Her father's voice was business-like. 'Look, my dear, Robin isn't reacting quite as well as we'd hoped. Pulmonary infection has developed and the little chap is having a tough time. He's showing signs of delirium and keeps calling for "Susy". It must be you. I wondered if you'd like to get down here. There's a chance that it might help him. Ross is due in a half an hour or so, but I'm sure he'd agree with me that your presence could only be to the good.'

'Well, Dad, I don't know. . .' She knew she shouldn't be hesitating.

'Susy, I'm not asking you to do a long spell of duty, simply to perform a humane act for a small boy who needs the one person with whom he feels some sort of real affinity. Won't you do it, darling? I thought it was something you would jump at.'

'Yes, Dad, I know what you mean, but would. . . would Ross approve, and Miss Aldridge, the SNO?' The mere thought of being on the periphery of the system set her heart pounding.

'Just leave all those considerations to me, Susy. Now if you really feel that you can come over, please do so and I'll square the rest.'

Her mouth was dry as she said quickly before changing her mind, 'Right, Dad, I'll leave now.'

The Jersey General was brilliantly lit as Susy drove the car into the car park; it was nine o'clock now, visitors were leaving everywhere and the place was a hive of activity. Swiftly she parked and made her way over to the paediatric unit. It was still as yet largely unmanned but as she stepped into the reception area a voice greeted her. 'Miss Frenais! How nice! We were expecting you; it's so good of you to help us out like this. I do hope it's not too much of an inconvenience?'

Miss Margaret Aldridge, a very youthful-looking forty-year-old, came from her office. Her well-fitting navy blue uniform dress enhanced a very trim figure; she had short brown hair and a round, small-featured face with a pleasant smile, which immediately made Susy feel that she really was welcome.

Susy took a deep breath. 'Hello, Miss Aldridge. I'm only too glad to be here. I just hope that Robin's going to respond as we expect.'

'I'm sure he will. Come along into my office, my dear, and I'll just give you an apron in case. What a warm night it is. Do come in.'

In the shiny new intensive care unit, the little boy lay with closed eyes, the dusting of freckles across his nose showing up in contrast to the pale soft skin. Dark copper curls clung damply to his brow, and an oxygen mask covered the lower part of his features.

'He's already had an injection to help relieve the congestion, but. . .' Miss Aldridge shook her head anxiously.

Gently touching Robin's small hand on the coverlet, Susy heard the door open and her father came in. 'Miss Aldridge. . . Susy! So glad you're here. Little progress by the look of things,' Ian Frenais said, glancing at the chart, then at Miss Aldridge.

'I think he seems a little less restive now, sir.'

'Yes. Well, I'm off home now. Ross has just arrived, so no doubt he'll be along to check how things are.' He smiled at them both, then back at his daughter. 'I'm quite sure you'll soon be finding your way around, Susy. Goodnight now, but ring if you need me.'

Once Miss Aldridge had handed her Robin's complete notes to read, Susy found herself alone in the room with only the slight hiss of air being inhaled and expelled. She became absorbed by the notes, concerned at the swiftness with which Robin's illness had overtaken him. Starting with a diagnosis of influenza, he had quickly succumbed to a potentially acute attack of either asthma or pneumonia, perhaps both.

Vaguely she heard the soft click of the door behind her. Ross had appeared at the other side of the child's bed, giving her a curt nod, before saying quietly, 'Glad you're here, Susy. Your father gave me all the gen. about Robin calling for you.'

'Yes, I don't know if I managed to get through to him when I spoke earlier, but at the moment he seems to be in a light sleep.'

'Can I see his notes, please?'

She passed them to him, sensing a very faint suggestion of command about him, as if now it required a completely different attitude from him towards her. She studied the child's flushed face, as Ross murmured relevant comments while studying the charts. 'Mmm, the most essential thing now is to assess the severity of airflow obstruction and its components. It could only be bronchitis as yet and not pneumonia.' He sighed, a small frown between his dark brows. 'But without the normal home background it's difficult to know if there was ever any pre-existent lung disease.'

Susy smoothed the boy's hair back from his damp forehead. 'Do you think that the recent excitement he's had when I've taken him out, or fear of the outings coming to an end, could have any bearing on the ferocity of this attack? It certainly came upon him very quickly.'

Ross shook his head. 'Very difficult to know. However, your presence has obviously helped; he seems quieter now.'

After Ross left, Susy stayed on with the child at Miss Aldridge's request for the next two hours, taking a break for a meal and then returning to the ICU for a further spell. She was still there some time after midnight, hardly realising just how tired she was when to her surprise Ross came back, dark hair ruffled, lines of strain about his face as he took a look at the sleeping child, and murmured softly, 'Sorry I couldn't get in before. We've had an emergency admittance of a cot-death baby. No hope for him, I'm afraid.' He pushed a hand through his hair. 'God, it's such a tragic business. The parents are distraught, of course.'

'Can I help?' Susy asked, quite forgetting she wasn't in her normal environment.

'Not now, thanks. The parents-in-law have just turned up, and Miss Aldridge is looking after them. Incidentally, we've only two other young trainee nurses on duty tonight, apart from the SNO. He gave her a half-smile, pinching the bridge of his nose, closing his eyes briefly, saying, 'But we'll manage as usual.'

She was surprised to hear herself say, 'You look as if you can do with some sleep. I can stay on until the day staff arrive if it would help.'

He gave her a grateful smile. 'Thank you, I'm sure Miss Aldridge would be only too delighted with the offer.' He glanced at Robin's quietly sleeping form. 'Why not go along to the main building and get yourself coffee and a sandwich? Meanwhile I'll ring Miss Aldridge and tell her.'

Susy stayed on until six the following morning, having given Robin a bronchodilator by injection at regular intervals. She checked his pulse for any sign of an increase in rate or rhythm. At some time in the early morning hours, she was so worried when Robin showed signs of restlessness and fear again that she rang

Ross, who instructed that a further injection of hydro-cortisone should be given.

'Susy. . . Susy. . .' the husky young voice whispered pitifully in the silent room.

She took his hand in hers, murmuring gently in reassurance, 'I'm here, Robin; you're going to have a nice sleep now. You're going to be so much better in the morning.'

'Can we go. . .to the beach?'

'Yes, of course, once you're better.'

'Games. . .?' The small voice became fainter as the deep sleep took over, his small fingers curling around hers in complete and utter confidence.

'Yes, darling,' she whispered. 'Lots and lots more.'

Susy had no idea how long she stayed at his bedside. Ross must have come and gone again at some time, and all she remembered when the light of day was already showing was trying to rouse herself from a tired stupor into which she had dropped for two or three minutes from sheer exhaustion.

'Morning, Miss Frenais!' The voice pulled her together with a start, as she smiled.

'Morning!' A cup of tea was put into her hand. A day staff nurse was grinning at her, one whom she recognised as a friend of Julia's. 'Thanks, this is great!'

'You certainly look whacked. Miss Aldridge told me you were here. She says you've got to get off home straight away!'

'Wow! This tea's like nectar! Well, I must say I'm looking forward to my bed, thanks.'

'I see the little boy's temp appears to have dropped during the night, then.'

Susy studied Robin's calmer features. 'Yes, fingers crossed, and I think with luck we might avoid pneumonia.'

'Poor little kid; he was really rough when he first came in, but Dr Beaumaris kept a good watch over

him. I just don't know what we'd do without that man;
he comes in at all hours of the day and night if
necessary for "his" children, you know.'

Susy drove home in the early morning sun feeling as if
a great burden had fallen from her shoulders despite
her tiredness. It was the sheer joy of being back amid
the world of the job she knew and loved that swept
over her, and for nearly twelve hours her mind had
been completely absorbed and set on Robin's recovery
over and above everything else. She ran the car window
down, smelling the fresh tang of the sea as the incoming
tide rippled and shone in the bright light; the beach
below the cliff road looked clean and golden, and
briefly she burst out into song with the wonderful
feeling of being herself again. No longer any tunnel of
grief to fight her way through, no aching misery for
Patrick and longing for his presence that now could
never be. Twelve hours of complete and utter freedom!
She knew it couldn't last; nevertheless, hadn't her
mother said this was how it would be: a gradual
adaptation to another way of living and another life?
    Her buoyancy began to deflate very slightly when
she remembered Ross Beaumaris, and his slightly aloof
attitude towards her at first in the hospital. It was only
a momentary thing, but even worse was the initial
tremble of fear she had felt when he first entered
Robin's room. Again that awful sense of lost confidence, which she prayed had not shown. Still, all of
that passed subsequently, and for the rest of the time it
was just great to be back in the swim — if only briefly.
As she drew up outside the cottage she remembered
too that nothing more had been said about her returning to the hospital. However, she could no longer
worry. Her mind whirled with tiredness as she went
indoors, and her mother was already up and about
preparing breakfast.

'Hello, darling,' Dorothy greeted Susy with a smile. 'How did you get on?'

Over breakfast she and Susy, and later her father, discussed Robin's chances of a good recovery; but little else once her eyes refused to remain open. Upstairs she slept better than she had for some time. Hours later, it seemed, she awoke to late afternoon sunlight streaming through the drawn curtains. For a while she lay in her bed, dazzled by the brilliance, collecting her thoughts which had already taken an optimistic turn since her body and mind had rested. Domestic sounds came to her ears: the barking of Bill and Ben, their King Charles spaniels; the kitchen radio; the whirr of a lawnmower. Such ordinary, homely things which poor little Robin might never know in his young life. Her mother had mentioned the possibility of fostering and adoption for childen at the home, and the thought sent a sharp pang of anxiety through her, having developed an unaccountable wave of possessiveness for the child.

Hurriedly she left her bed, curbing her mixed emotions which could serve no purpose, certainly not at that moment when a shower was far more to the point. The phone rang just as she finished washing her hair; winding a thick towel around it, she picked up the instrument. 'Hello, Susy Frenais. . .'

'Ross here, Susy, hope I didn't disturb you?'

'No, I'm up and about!'

'Good. I wanted to thank you for putting in those extra hours with Robin; it seems to have helped greatly. I was very surprised and pleased to see the improvement this morning.'

'I'm so glad, Ross. I must say I was relieved; I still feel he was in need of reassurance.'

'You're probably right. Look—um—I have to go away on business to London, also I'm meeting the American friend I told you about at Heathrow. This whole thing's going to take just a couple of days and I

wondered if you would come over to the hospital to
see Robin again and spend a little time with him? It
would also give you the opportunity to meet the rest of
the staff and get to know both them and the surroundings more thoroughly, seeing that changes have been
made. . .'

'Thank you, Ross,' Susy said, trying not to sound
panicked. 'By all means I'll come if you think Robin
needs me.'

'Well, that's splendid! Now remember there's no
pressure at all. I've had a word with Miss Aldridge and
she's in favour too if you feel up to it, but I must leave
that for you to decide. There's nothing permanent
about any of it; just do whichever appeals to you most.'

'Right.' She took a deep breath. 'No doubt I'll be
seeing Robin after getting in touch with Miss Aldridge.'

'Fine; see you when I get back.'

Slowly she replaced the phone, the towel dropping
from her hair leaving long damp strands releasing soft
tendrils drying about her face as she sat pondering
upon Ross's words. She was, deep down, still hesitant
to agree to his request immediately even though it was
for Robin, and yet while at the hospital with him the
night before she would have stayed indefinitely had he
needed her. The crazy, wayward thought even crossed
her mind; what sort of answer would she have given
had he suggested she apply for the appointment of
sister in the new unit? She shrugged the words away; it
was all so much daydreaming when there were still the
subconscious tensions continuing to haunt her. Nevertheless, things were improving, she was sure of that,
but it wasn't going to happen overnight.

She finished her hair then dressed, still dwelling on
her thoughts, and when a certain calm had settled over
her she rang Miss Aldridge and thanked her for agreeing with Ross about Robin, and also enquired after the
child's progress.

'He's still improving, Susy,' came the pleasant reply. 'If he carries on this way we're going to put him in with the other children in the main ward. We already have two young patients there, and I think it'll be good for him. Might you be coming in today for a while?'

'Well, yes. Is this afternoon convenient?'

'Perfect! We are always so glad of any help we can get. Susy, why not pop in to the office and see me before you go on to the ward this afternoon?'

'Yes, I'll do that, Miss Aldridge,' Susy said, rather apprehensively, hoping the SNO didn't want to change things from the voluntary basis under which she was expecting to work at present; foolishly perhaps, but she looked upon the present arrangement as a possible 'escape route' should a recurrence of her problem suddenly become too much.

Miss Aldridge was her usual charming self when Susy sat down in her office. 'Now, Susy,' she said warmly, 'I've been thinking. As you know we're always so very glad of any general help we can get, apart, that is, from what you are doing with Robin, and it occurred to me that from now on you might like to help out with the normal daily work, yet at the same time reassuring Robin that you were on hand? You see, it might well be better not to have him thinking that you were there specifically for his benefit. As you know, children are very quick to spot this sort of thing, particularly as he has now turned the corner of his illness. . .' She smiled wisely.

'Um. . .well, I——'

Miss Aldridge broke in gently. 'I don't want you to worry about this, my dear; it's just a proposal and must be entirely your decision, and, just so long as you let me know each morning you are able to come here, that's all I ask. You will of course be at liberty to work as and when is suitable for you.'

Susy felt a sudden rush of warmth at the SNO's vote

of confidence in her, which immediately boosted her own morale tremendously, as she heard herself agreeing readily to what the kindly woman had put to her.

Subsequently, it was no surprise whatsoever to Susy that it took less than the first hour on the ward of the new unit to confirm that her impulsive decision was the right one.

It was as if all faltering despair had vanished as soon as she entered the environment that to her was as natural as living and breathing. If only the feeling would remain and be wholly dependable. . . But she quickly thrust the thoughts from her, and when one of the two young students working on the ward asked brightly if she was working the following morning as well as that afternoon Susy's heart welled up with a kind of thankfulness to Rosa, the rosy-faced young girl, which made her reply utterly spontaneous. 'Well, Miss Aldridge suggested I come in at any time to help on the wards as well as with Robin, and I'd really love to.'

The girl beamed. 'Terrific! We all know that Robin wants to see you, and you're great with the other children, Susy. I heard Dr Beaumaris telling Matron at the home what a difference it had made.'

The following morning, Robin certainly seemed to be improving and his eyes followed her everywhere. She read stories, coaxed him to eat a little, washed him, brushed his curls, and carried out all the medical and pratical requirements of a sick child returning to normal.

That afternoon he had been watching her put the finishing touches to making his bed while cuddling Puff, his small teddy-bear. The child's eyes were quite drowsy and Susy was convinced he was trying to fend off a cat-nap. But no; instead, he had apparently been thinking very hard when he said suddenly, 'Susy, why are you wearing that funny apron? The other nurses wear different clothes.'

'That's because I'm not always here as they are.'

'Would you always be here if you could get some proper clothes like that, then?'

'I don't think so, darling!' Susy laughed. 'Dr Ross would have something to say, I imagine. Now, how about you having a little snooze? I'll read you a story first, shall I?'

'OK, but when can I go and play with the others?'

'Very soon now. Miss Aldridge and Dr Ross will decide that.'

'Dr Ross isn't here,' he said with all the peevish impatience of a convalescent child.

'It won't be long now, Robin. You have a little sleep, then I wouldn't be surprised if there's something special for tea.'

'But it won't be like Aunty Dorothy's, though, will it?'

Susy darted back to the bed playfully, hand on hips. 'Robin Masters, you sound like Grumpy, one of the Seven Dwarfs we were reading about, do you know that?'

Robin chuckled almost against his will, but he had the last word. 'Well, I haven't got a long white beard, have I?'

Susy was still smiling to herself when she left the ICU to return to the main ward. It was small, with its intended quota for six, but contained enough playthings, games and books for dozens of children, as well as a huge rocking horse that was rarely still. While helping to prepare teas, Susy wondered if Ross had yet met his friend arriving from America, and what he was like. When the two men returned to Jersey she only hoped the friend would not expect her to supply statistics and analyses of the Belfast children and their lifestyle, as well as the nursing side of her time there, when it had been nothing but work, sleep and eat. But for Patrick, she would have had little or no social life at all.

Later, giving a hand with two beds for new admissions that afternoon, she made a supreme effort to shrug off the worrying mood she had fallen into, and was rather glad when the office phone rang. It was Matron from the children's home.

'Hello, Mrs Harris,' Susy said. 'I'm afraid there's only two young nurses and myself here at present.'

'Not to worry, my dear. It was Miss Aldridge's secretary who put me through to you as the SNO wasn't available. I just wanted a word on Robin's progress.'

'Good news, Mrs Harris. In fact he's made great strides.'

'That's marvellous. I've been hearing how much your help's been appreciated with Robin. I'll ring off now, and thank you again.'

Two afternoons later, Susy had just finished changing bedlinen with Rosa's help when vaguely she heard the sound of men's voices in the corridor. The first thing that crossed her mind was that Ross might be back with his friend. The thought of seeing Ross so suddenly hit her with both pleasure and apprehension as the sound grew nearer. She was right. It was him. Now, as her heart beat faster, she couldn't forget the slightly superior air he had adopted when she'd first helped out with Robin. Her cheeks felt hot as the familiar voice grew even nearer. Fortunately her back was turned while she attempted to take down the usual sweetie jar from the cupboard produced as one of the many highlights of the children's day. But, instead of Ross Beaumaris, another vaguely familiar tone in an American tongue called out in surprise, 'Say! I'd know that lovely back-view anywhere! It just has to be Susy. Remember me, honey?'

She swung round, putting the jar aside before the contents scattered all over the floor, suddenly coming face to face with the tall, good-looking man now beaming back at her. Then it clicked.

'Marc!' she gasped incredulously. 'Oh, Marc!'

CHAPTER FIVE

STILL stunned with surprise, Susy looked into the face of the boyish, mid-forties, broad-shoulderd doctor of whom she'd thought so often. Now he grasped both her hands in his, friendship and admiration shining from his dark brown eyes. 'Well, I'm darned, Susy; I never thought I'd track you down here!'

They'd met and worked together in Casualty so briefly through two of the worst days in Belfast that had seemed like a lifetime, stopping only for coffee, with spells of duty going on long into the night that had turned them into lifelong friends in less than forty-eight hours. Now the delighted expression in his eyes made tears start in her own as all the memories came flooding back.

'Marc! I'd no idea that Ross was talking about you when he said his friend was visiting.'

Ross, standing to one side, appeared to be summing up the situation, pleasure and puzzlement in his eyes. 'Well, it seems to be an even smaller world than I thought! Fancy the two of you already knowing each other!'

Marc, his Italian American blood revealing itself in the dark hair and eyes and swarthy complexion of his race, laughed happily. 'Ross, Susy and I have just got to find time to get together; this is someone I thought never to see again! In fact, I was hell-bent on trying to find her while I was here. Oh, boy, this really is terrific, Susy!'

She still appeared somewhat speechless, although the meeting appeared to have afflicted Marc in quite the other way. She was not unaware either that Ross

still looked slightly nonplussed, perhaps suddenly realising that he was not going to have his friend's
undivided attention. 'Ross,' she said rather breathlessly
by way of explanation, 'it must be over two years since
Marc was at our hospital on one of his surveys, and he
got caught up with us on just about one of the worst
bomb outrages in Belfast they'd known in a very long
time.'

'I sure did,' Marc joined in. 'God, the way those
people at the hospital worked the two nights I was
there, I'll never forget it in the whole of my life. I can
tell you, Ross, I'm ashamed to confess I was pretty
glad to get the hell out of there, that's for sure!' He
grinned at Susy. 'And consequently although Susy and
I were together all those hours we'd hardly had time to
know more than each other's first names, let alone
exchange addresses. I certainly won't let that happen
again. We sure do have a whole lot of news to catch up
on.' He turned to Ross with a grin. 'Say, fella, you're
one lucky guy having this gorgeous gal working for
you. She can come back to the States and do the same
for me any time!'

Susy's cheeks burned with embarrassment and she
said quickly, 'Marc, you were certainly doing your
share those dreadful nights, as I'm sure Ross realises.'

'Not true, honey,' he said quickly. 'Well, if it's OK
workwise, how about having dinner with me tomorrow
night? Ross and I will be going over old times tonight
at his place and there's no telling what time we'll be
through. My old buddy here usually has some decent
Scotch, as I recall, and I'm really looking forward to
that. So what do you say, honey? I'll take a cab and
come out to your place to pick you up, then we'll eat
at my hotel—how's that?' He grinned. 'Adjani's the
name, Marc Adjani. And you're. . .?'

'Susy Frenais,' she murmured, still over-conscious of
Ross's presence as she added spontaneously, 'Thanks,

Marc, that'll be terrific!' How could she possibly refuse?

The two men eventually completed the tour of the unit and then went on to the SNO's office where tea was served, and Susy could still hear the loud, genial tones of Marc's voice as she left the hospital and drove away for home, her mind a kaleidoscope of fragmentary thoughts almost impossible to sort out, and which stayed with her the entire evening.

Next morning Susy was on her way back from the lab to collect some blood samples. Her head was in the clouds; she had actually felt confident enough to go there and ask for what she wanted without feeling nervously self-conscious. A small errand, she knew, yet another pointer that indicated that the tension was leaving her at a time when she so needed, longed, to record mentally every small important step forward of her progress.

Crossing the main reception hall, she caught a brief glimpse of Ross, standing relaxed and very self-possessed as he laughed and talked with one of the more senior women doctors. Susy made to go through the old-style double doors into a vestibule where the automatic doors slid open into the new wing, when she heard him call.

'Susy, can I have a word?'

She stopped in her tracks as he walked briskly towards her. 'Hi, Ross.'

'I'm coming along to the ward. I wanted to see young Kevin Stannard, the four-year-old. Lively little boy.'

She gave a small frown of concentration. 'The one you operated on about nine days ago for the neck?'

They carried on walking into the unit. 'That's the one.' He smiled, as the sound of laughter and shouting welcomed them on their way past the kiddies' playroom. 'I want to remove his stitches shortly, but before doing so I thought you might like to know a little about the case. It's really quite interesting.'

He glanced at her quickly, thinking how much more relaxed she looked during the time spent at the hospital. He hadn't yet voiced his thoughts to anyone else, but it was his intention to try and draw Susy out of herself. Whatever this block was that had so badly restricted her potential, he was determined to encourage her and try to help remove the pain of her suffering, whether mental or physical. 'Now,' he went on, not waiting for her reply, 'the boy's op was to correct a congenital condition sometimes known as "wry neck", due to spasm in the neck muscles. The poor kid has to hold his head constantly to one side after passive, gentle stretching does not respond. Quite often it's due to a kinking of the neck before birth. The swelling that sometimes develops has now been corrected by surgery, and later further passive stretchings and active exercise will take place when the boy is up and about.'

'Is this whole thing usually successful? He's always such a cheerful little soul.'

'I know, he has built-in optimism!' They stopped at the child's bed, and Ross beamed at him. 'And how's the little demon this morning?' Ross chuckled, while glancing at his bed chart.

Kevin giggled, and appealed to Susy. 'I'm not a little demon, am I, Susy? I'm good,' the youngster declared. He certainly was, having had to lie on his bed in the over-corrected position, a folded hand-towel acoss his forehead and the head held by sandbags of suitable size placed on the ends of the towel. Nor had he been allowed to sit up for nine days, as well as being washed and fed by staff when his parents were not always able to be there.

Susy glanced at Ross in jest. 'Well, Dr Ross, what do you think — shall we change our minds?'

Ross's eyes crinkled at the sides as he laughed. 'Why not? What about a little rogue instead?'

Kevin basked in all the teasing and extra attention, thoroughly enjoying himself. 'Will I be able to get up soon, then, Dr Ross?'

'Very soon, old chap. In fact I might be in to see you again this afternoon.' Ross grinned as he strolled away to the two other children recently admitted for Still's Disease, and who would be spending some time lying full-length in plaster beds. 'Hello, you two! Would you believe it — I've forgotten your names! I hope you can tell me!'

'I'm Barry!' called the small young blond rascal with a riot of curls and dark brown eyes.

'I'm Tom,' piped up blue-eyed, dark-haired Tom Thumb, the name given him by his mother since birth as a prem.

'Tell Susy how old you are as well,' Ross prompted.

'Three!' They shouted in unison, convulsed in laughter when Ross and Susy pretended to jump from their skin.

'Well, boys, are you comfortable?'

'No!'

'Yes!'

'Oh, dear, I think I shall have to find out from Mrs Wallis, the physiotherapist; she'll be in this morning to make certain you're OK. I'll see you later. Be good!'

As they walked back to the office, Ross murmured with a sigh, 'Poor little devils. The treatment is slow but, I contend, far better in plaster beds than separate splints on limbs and having to spend time often flat on their face from time to time. At least the plaster method is effective against preventing contracture-deformities too.'

'But their general health will gradually improve?'

'Oh, indeed, but these children need years of skilled and knowledgeable care.' He glanced at his wristwatch.

'I'm afraid I must fly. I've a meeting before lunch.' He gave her a swift look. 'You're not finding all this too tiring?'

'No, not a bit,' she laughed, touched by his thoughtfulness.

'Good. Susy, I've rather a busy schedule this afternoon but I intend trying to get back here if I can and wheedling Staff Nurse Mason on Medical to spare me a hand briefly. It's not desperately essential, tomorrow would do, but as the children have been so good I thought I'd try and get back anyway.'

'There's no doubt they'd be thrilled!'

After Ross had gone, Susy carried on happily, helping with the children's lunch, and when the two student nurses returned from the canteen after having their own she left the ward to do the same, and ran into Miss Aldridge.

'Hello, Susy. I've been so busy this last few days I haven't had time to ask how you're getting along.'

'Well, if the rest of the staff are not finding it too much, I'm enjoying it immensely!'

'Splendid. Dr Beaumaris keeps me in touch and I think he's very pleased. Remember, though, we don't want your father saying we're wearing you out!'

'No fear of that,' Susy laughed as they parted company.

In the bright, airy canteen she collected a lasagne and coffee, carrying it to a corner window where she could admire the newly waning summer now turning into a gentle autumn outside. Sunshine dappled the leaves in a variety of reds and gold, and for the first time she was able to recall, without misery, when Patrick and she had laughingly kicked their feet through carpets of colour in a beechwood forest near his home, hand in hand without a care in the world when they had first met. Now, she no longer dashed the memory swiftly from her mind for fear of tears, but it simply warmed her heart to remember such fragments of happiness to be coveted for all time.

'Can I join you?' asked a warm, friendly voice. Staff Nurse Hilary Mason, a medium-height, sturdy girl, with dark curly hair and stern face — until she smiled — stood there. 'It's Susy Frenais, isn't it?' she said, putting down her tray.

'Hi, yes! Take a seat, do!'

'Thanks. It's been chaotic lately and I haven't had five minutes to get to know you, not that Julia hasn't kept me informed! How are you enjoying helping out here?'

'Great so far, thanks. Everyone's so nice.'

'Well, I had to say I had selfish reasons as well for barging in like this, Susy. It's our Dr Beaumaris, I wondered if you knew whether he's coming back to the unit this afternoon. When he told me after his round that there was a possibility, I didn't know if you'd heard anything more specific.'

'No, not really, except that he mentioned vaguely he'd like to see the children later, if possible.'

'Oh, well, it can't have been much. It was just the way he hinted he rather wanted me to stand by when he turned up. I'll be around somewhere, anyway, so he can always send up a rocket.'

Back on the ward it was the 'quiet hour' before visitors arrived; parents came at any time and knew that the 'ortho' children were always fairly subdued or in need of a short sleep at that spot in the day so it was comparatively calm when Susy returned, except for one or two older children in the playroom who had been allowed up that morning.

With such an ideal opportunity Susy decided to do some filing in the office, grateful that the new unit comprised such a haven rather than the more usual open 'station', particularly when Ross popped his head around the door suddenly.

'Got away earlier than I thought.' He grinned

amiably. 'I've just been along for a word with Hilary, and she's rather tied up at the moment and can't do that small job I had in mind, so I wondered if you'd help out, Susy.'

'If I can,' she said lightly, pushing the files aside.

'Good. Well, I'd like you to remove young Kevin's stitches for me.'

Susy stared into the dark blue eyes, wondering if her hearing was faulty. 'Sorry, Ross, I didn't quite catch what you said.' Her heart had begun the slow, thumping beat she knew so well, as if she were pounding along for her life. She heard Ross repeat the same words, and mumbled hoarsely, 'Oh, I don't think I should, Ross. I mean. . . I'm not. . .not. . .on the staff. It might not even be ethical.'

He burst into a gale of laughter, saying quickly, 'Hey, Susy, leave me to worry about permission; the buck stops here —' he tapped his chest ' — with me, remember?' He swung round quickly to one of the student nurses who at that moment was passing the open door. 'You already have a suture trolley laid up, haven't you, Rosa? Yes, good. Take it along to young Kevin's bed, will you, please? We'll be there in a couple of minutes.' His face was businesslike suddenly as he thrust a hand out towards Susy. 'I'll have the boy's file, please, Susy, then we'll get on.'

Susy had gone numb, and her legs felt the same. She was acting like a puppet on a string. It was impossible; she couldn't do this job. Suddenly they reached Kevin's bedside. . .

Ross gave Kevin a huge grin. 'Hi, Kevin! Today's the day, then, heh? We'll make this the big moment to remove those stitches, shall we?'

'Yeah, then I can get up, can't I?'

'All in good time, my lad. Susy will take those stitches out and then we'll see how well you're doing.'

'Will it hurt?'

'Definitely not. Susy is one of the best people I could get for removing stitches; she's magic, I can tell you!'

As Ross was speaking, it was slowly dawning upon Susy that for the first time in months she was faced with a job that required skill and nerve; nerve particularly, after a prolonged absence from doing such things. Only vaguely did she hear Ross's light-hearted comments as she removed the dressings, for the result of the operation could be a big step forward towards the child's head growing into the correct position and giving him a normal future.

Her mouth was dry and her heart thumped. If she did not handle this job well and with confidence, all her other hesitant longings to return to work would be of no avail. She prayed that her hands would not shake, so conscious was she of Ross's eyes upon her as he stood at her shoulder. For a moment, as the newly healed wound revealed itself and she saw the neat stitches waiting to be removed, a red mist seemed to swim across her eyes and she wanted to turn and run. But a movement on the other side of the bed from Rosa, watching with awed respect, and Kevin's large eyes upon her with all the confidence that Ross had instilled in him, steadied the world around her. The only other thing was a sudden pall of silence from the other children in the ward that hung like a huge presence.

Rosa held out the galley dish containing forceps and scissors, waiting patiently as Susy's slim fingers touched the metal objects, causing a clatter which seemed loud enough to deafen, but at the same time pulled her out from some of the longest seconds of her entire life. She took a deep breath. Her mind cleared. She was back in Belfast, an orthopaedic sister performing a routine job, cool, calm and collected with never a doubtful moment over anything she had to do for which she'd been trained. Patrick's faith in her was suddenly a living thing.

With a firm hand now, Susy removed the sutures cleanly and painlessly, each one falling in to the dish like small individual triumphs towards her ultimate goal of taking up the reins of work again. She bent over the child to remove the final stitch, then straightened up, and with an inward sigh of relief and satisfaction gave Kevin a conspiratorial wink. 'There we are, Kevin; you didn't feel a thing, did you?'

'No, but that's what Dr Ross said,' came the childish logic of belief in adults. 'Can I get up now, please?'

'Teatime first!'

She walked back with Ross, neither saying anything except that he murmured before leaving, 'Well done, Susy. That job was equal to Staff Nurse Mason any day, but don't tell her I said so!'

Her heart sang for the rest of the day; nothing could dishearten her, not even the sudden influx of late visitors.

Soon afterwards Rosa and herself, on Ross's instructions, assisted young Kevin to take his first steps after what must have been to him endless days of inactivity for one so naturally boisterous. It was only the beginning, and ultimately, after a few steps around his bed, returning him to it without all the medical paraphernalia of the last ten days was equally exciting for him. While he was relishing the newness of his little world, his bright young face animated, he said brightly, 'Can I sit up now for a long time, Nurse, and look at my books?'

'Of course you can, Kevin,' Susy said, packing pillows comfortably at his back, and fastening a medical collar at his neck, padded higher on the affected side more to remind him to keep his head straight from now on than anything else. 'And when I see you tomorrow we'll go for an even longer walk.'

Kevin's face lit up suddenly. 'Robin! Hi! Come and talk to me.'

Susy hadn't noticed that Rosa had been given permission to wheel the boy in, in his chair, to the orthopaedic side to have his lunch with the other children. 'Robin! Hello, I didn't know you were there! My word, you were quiet!'

Robin beamed, colour filling his cheeks. 'I was sitting here watching Kevin, and you didn't see me!'

'My goodness, fancy me doing that!' Susy laughed.

'When you take Kevin for a walk tomorrow, Susy, can I come too?'

He'd obviously misunderstood what sort of walk it was going to be, but it didn't matter for he looked quite happy. 'We'll see what Dr Ross says, Robin. You can stay with Kevin for a little while now if you want to.'

Susy didn't see Ross again before she went off duty later that afternoon, and she wondered if he'd remembered that she was having dinner with Marc that night. She still felt conscience-stricken at taking up the time Ross had hoped to spend talking shop with his old friend, but there was not a lot she could do about it.

In the car park she saw Julia, who was just arriving for work. 'Hi! How are things?'

'Fine, thanks, Susy. I was really chuffed to hear about this temp work you've decided to do. Is it helping you make the decision not to give up? I jolly well hope so.'

Susy made a small grimace with her lips. 'Well, I'll admit to feeling better now that I'm more involved.'

Julia flung an arm around her friend's shoulders. 'Come on, now, that's the first big step forward, and don't you forget it! See you tomorrow perhaps!'

As Susy drove home, she remembered she hadn't told Julia she was going out with Marc that evening. It could be that Julia still didn't know who he was—

visitors were always coming and going, VIPs particularly — but she'd certainly tell her later, and, knowing Julia, she was sure to say it was just what Susy needed!

Marc's hotel was situated just outside St Helier where the best rooms overlooked the sea and the public ones all had vistas of rolling countryside with occasional sight of inlets, and small channels of water where luxury boats were tied up at the bottom of equally luxurious gardens. In the dining-room Marc and Susy had finished dinner, and over a centrepiece of cream roses sat listening to each other's news in eager, friendly affection. Marc poured them another cup of coffee, his light tropical suit immaculate, his manner laid-back, waiting to hear all she had to tell him. She stopped suddenly, and his look was quizzical as he said with a grin, 'You know, Susy, it's just great to have heard about the last two years since we met, but what about that engagement of yours? If you remember, you told me during one of our brief moments in Belfast. Is that still on?' His eyes had strayed to the third finger of her left hand, only a white circle on the tan skin where a ring used to be. Now it hung on a gold chain against her heart which he'd noticed when helping her off with her jacket earlier.

She had been waiting for the question, and somehow knew instinctively that it was not going to be hard talking to Marc about it; in fact she almost welcomed it. 'It's all over, Marc,' she said quietly. 'It happened a few months after you left. Things have never been the same since.' She told him the whole story from beginning to end, holding nothing back. Even when her words stumbled and her voice shook, he didn't interrupt, only the worried sympathy in his eyes enough to convince her of his thoughts. 'And so, the point is now, Marc, far from being home on holiday, I've really been sent back on leave because I was firmly convinced that my nursing days were over.'

'And now?' he asked gently.

She glanced down at the primrose-yellow cloth, then to the long windows beside them where a light sea-mist was settling in with the approach of dusk over the late summer countryside. 'I honestly don't know, Marc; it's all been so traumatic. I'm supposedly convalescent following a nervous breakdown. As I said, I kept going for a year after Patrick's death, refusing to believe it, determined to carry on as if nothing had happened so that perhaps eventually my mind would absorb it and I'd get on with my life as before.'

'But it doesn't work that way, does it?' Marc said soberly. 'I can't tell you how sorry I am this has happened, Susy — it's the last thing I expected to hear — but how come my first sighting of you was working in the peds ward this time?'

'Well, as you know, Dad's at the hospital. . .' She told him about the children at the home, as well as the shortage of staff at the hospital. She gave a wry smile. 'I was drawn back despite myself, I suppose, but. . . but my big worry all along had been that if I took another "proper" job away from Belfast I wouldn't fully regain my confidence. It's a dreadful feeling, Marc, when one's been in a position of responsibility, suddenly to realise that all belief in oneself seems unattainable.'

'Did you have counselling at Belfast?'

'I've been asked that here, too. I always give the same answer. I thought I could resolve it for myself, but once I got home I discovered it was far more difficult than I'd imagined. I even broke out into a cold sweat crossing the threshold of our local hospital where I'd partly trained — a terrifying experience.'

Marc sat silently for a few seconds, his kindly features serious as if he was miles away. 'Susy,' he said suddenly. 'There has never been time for me to talk either, certainly not about private and personal things.

I only mention this now because you are an intelligent, talented and lovely girl, and I cannot, will not see such a person throw all that away. I know deep down inside somewhere you have the guts to take all of this. Patrick's death will only serve to strengthen it, believe me, I know.'

'You know?' she murmured.

'Yes,' he said bluntly, all the light-hearted humour gone from his voice. 'I'm forty-five years old, Susy, and twenty years ago I fell in love with a girl at college and we married as soon as we'd graduated. Life was beautiful; no two people could ever have been so happy. When there was a baby on the way we had everything. The time came for our child to be born, there were complications and both she and the baby died.' Marc's face was empty suddenly, his eyes a million miles away, but he went on, 'My whole world had crashed, and, like you, I thought I could carry on — had to carry on — but when I started drinking too much I needed to take myself in hand, and I tell you this — good though counselling can be — and I had some — in the end, I was the one who had to make that final decision. Either I had to throw up all my medical training, years of it, or fight for my dead wife and son's sake. That's what I did and never regretted it. I've never married again; never struck upon the sort of love I once had — not that I haven't tried a couple of times —' he smiled suddenly ' — but I guess when a standard's been set I'm the sort of guy who prefers to stick to it. But girl, don't let your work go; don't lose faith in something that you've wanted to do all your life — it's too precious. You'll win through, I just know you will.'

'Marc —' she could hardly speak for what she'd heard ' — what can I say? I'd no idea this terrible tragedy had happened to you, and yet you gave no hint when we all used to laugh so much together. I'm so sorry.'

'Look, honey, if you like to think of me as some kind of example, by all means do. I'm nothing special, but, if talking to me is going to help, for heaven's sake come to me at any time, certainly while I'm here in Jersey. I've another few weeks yet, longer than I first thought.'

'Thank you, Marc. Talking to you now has been a tonic. My parents know, and my friend Julia; other than that I've just felt I couldn't bear people's sympathy, well-intentioned though it is.'

'I know. . . I know. So Ross isn't aware of this either?'

'No. My father told him I'd had a stressful time in Belfast, and a broken engagement, and I. . .just left it at that.'

'You can depend on me not to say anything, Susy. That's for you to do when you're good and ready.'

Susy felt a rush of gratitude to this super man who had opened his heart to her. She stretched her hand out to touch his. 'Thank you, Marc, for everything tonight; it all means so much to me. You see, today at the hospital I removed some sutures from a wound — it was the first time in ages — and frankly I was absolutely terrified. But, to my joy, I overcame it and completed the job OK, and after what you've said I'm just hoping it means I've started to fight back because. . .'

'Because that's what you really want to do,' Marc smiled, finishing the sentence for her, and nodding with approval. 'That is *magnifico*, Susy! Now, I want you to promise me that we'll get together whenever we can to talk; talk about anything, but most of all about Patrick; Belfast; whatever. Not forgetting any progress such as today's. You'll get there, Susy, you're that kind of girl!'

She gave him a lovely smile. 'Marc, I bless the day we met in Belfast!'

'Talking of Belfast, honey, Ross and I will be going over there shortly for a couple of days to see how those kiddies are getting on. What I'm aiming to do is to try and get some of them over to the States to give them a holiday. What we're going to do is this. . .'

On the afternoon of the following day, Susy saw Ross arrive at the hospital and go into the office. Meanwhile, Rosa and herself carried on with the afternoon bed and bath routine before TPRs and medicines. There had been a sudden intake of six children on Medical with suspected food poisoning, and the two nurses were left to cope alone on Ortho. Nevertheless, her mind was still pleasantly content since her outing with Marc the night before, and snippets of what they had discussed constantly returned to her thoughts, like small gems to be treasured and stored away for when he had returned to the States.

Rosa and herself had only just finished when Ross came into the ward to see Kevin, who was happily immersed in a jigsaw puzzle. Ross gave Susy rather a formal smile, which made her wonder if he was annoyed about her going out with his friend. She tried to shrug aside the trivial thought. At least Ross was evidently pleased with Kevin's progress, but as he was leaving the ward he said casually, 'A word, please, Miss Frenais.'

Her heart did a double somersault. Had something gone wrong?

Ross addressed Susy curtly as they walked out and along the corridor. 'Come to Theatre, please, Miss Frenais. The last of the equipment's in place now, and I'd like you to check it over with me if you would. Then we can put final touches ready for the official opening next week. No doubt Marc told you we're off to Belfast tomorrow for a couple of days, so I don't want any last-minute hitches when I come back.'

In Theatre Ross waved a hand around the room, closing the door. 'Just take a look at that,' he said proudly. 'Isn't it splendid?'

She duly admired it, but, as they began checking and he was at her side, every now and again his body brushed close to hers. When they peered into one of the autoclaves, he was saying, 'I hope the chap's been in to see this thing; the pump was slightly faulty and steam pressure wasn't reaching the required hundred and twenty-five degrees Celsius reliably. That's one item to be checked.'

'Yes, I'll see to that.'

'The maintenance engineer might as well do a final OK on the air filters again, too. With so much technology everywhere, Susy, I want each member of staff eventually to become acquainted with most of the electrics in here.' He thrust his hands into his coat pockets. 'So, how did the dinner date go last night with Marc?'

She was rather caught off guard with the last question, having to select her words carefully about Marc. Also she was still very much aware of the magnetism drawing her to Ross, making it hard to concentrate upon what he was saying. It was as if whenever he was near she thought of all the wrong things; even the silly advertisement on TV she'd seen where sparks glowed between two hands had come to have some inane significance. She told herself it had happened since the day before when he had complimented her. From then on it had been difficult to think of him as a possible work colleague only, and she wondered in her saner moments if this was an offshoot of the loneliness she had tried to conceal. Now she answered his question breezily. 'Um. . .yes, it was a terrific evening, thanks. You can imagine we talked of Belfast most of the time.'

'I guessed that! You seem to have made quite an impression upon him.'

'I think in times of danger people's impressions can be rather exaggerated over a period.'

Ross smiled. 'I'm sure old Marc's a very sincere man!'

'He's certainly that,' she said with feeling.

Ross glanced at the clock. 'Almost time for you to be going off duty. Will you be doing another stint here again next week? I mean, you haven't planned any further job changes?'

'No. At the moment I'm quite happy to carry on temping while I'm needed.'

His dark eyes suddenly seared into hers, the sculptured mouth too close as he said in a low undertone, 'Oh, yes, you're. . .needed, believe me. . .'

In surprise at the intensity of his words, she tilted up her face to his, a quizzical look in her eyes, then momentarily the world seemed to fade around them, all motion suspended until his lips met hers, the pressure taking her breath away. She became too thrillingly aware of the tightening of his arms about her, the closeness of the hard-muscled frame. Then just as swiftly he stood her gently from him, his gaze sultry. 'That is a kiss of welcome for coming to work in the new unit, Susy. You've no idea how good it is to see you showing an interest in us, plus the fact that you are——' his eyes admired her '—quite an asset!' He was smiling now. 'In other words, you're looking so much better. I just hope you're enjoying being here?'

Her heart hammered; had his arms not been around her, her legs would not have been a lot of use, as she murmured more flippantly than she'd intended, 'How could I fail to?' She gave him a tantalising glance beneath her long lashes. 'The—um—staff are making it quite easy for me!'

'We do our best,' he laughed, then added more seriously, 'And all those doubts in your mind are getting short shrift, I hope?'

'Definitely.'

'Well, I have to say the children certainly love you. You deserve to know these things!'

'It all helps, Ross,' she grinned, near normality returning gradually.

'Do you ever do any sailing?' he asked, out of the blue, wondering if Marc had already beaten him to it.

Susy was about to answer when the intercom burst into life. 'Dr Beaumaris, please. Medical.'

He affected a groan. 'I'll reserve that last question for another time! Bye, now. . .' And he was gone.

She stood gazing into space and then thanked her lucky stars she was going home. Bestirring herself, she went out to the car, but couldn't stop thinking of Ross and his charmed manner, which included the kiss, though she banned that from her thoughts at present. Some of his other compelling characteristics — the basic kindliness, a need to please, and a sense of humour — she admired greatly on coming to know him better. Nevertheless, she still needed to be reminded of his attraction to other women, but as far as she was concerned she was sure he meant nothing more than an extremely pleasant friend and colleague. It did no harm either to remember that only that morning she had seen him along the corridor laughing down into the sultry eyes of Rebecca Cohen in much the same way as he had with herself that very afternoon.

While Susy drove home, her subconscious pounded in common sense where it was needed. Chemistry between two people was the very devil, she decided, particularly if the other person was totally unaware of it. Briefly, Patrick came into mind, and as she neared home she realised there had been very little anguish of this kind when she first knew him; it had all been so smooth and easy. If ever she began a new relationship with anyone ever again, wouldn't that be preferable?

At home her mother seemed to be in a high state of

excitement. 'Hi, Mum!' Susy called, going into the kitchen. 'You look about sixteen. Something nice happened?'

'Hello, darling, yes, it has. Your father came in at lunchtime with ideas of he and I going off on a cruise! I couldn't believe my ears. After all this time, he's actually decided to take a holiday!'

'That's terrific! Where to?'

'We haven't got that far yet. Mustn't tempt Fate!'

That evening she was on the patio with her parents, the sun shone, and the sea looked boisterous, making her think of her parents' holiday which had earlier been under discussion, while they had the drinks her father had poured.

'Have you ever thought of working here in Jersey permanently, Susy?' he said suddenly. Carefully he replaced the whisky stopper and came and sat beside her.

'No, Dad, not really. It could have flitted through my mind, but not with any seriousness.'

'Is there any appeal to you, for instance, if I suggested a new job at the unit?'

'How do you mean, Dad?'

'Well, don't misunderstand me, dear, I don't want to place any pressure upon you; you've had a damned hard time and you're at home here to make a complete recovery, and only you can be the judge of that. However, Miss Aldridge and I, and indeed Ross, are delighted at the way you've fitted in recently at work, and although the others have no idea what I've been thinking it occurred to me you may like to consider applying for the job of staff nurse at the peds unit. Looking ahead, provided things have gone satisfactorily, you could be ready to step straight into promotion to sister. Of course, the hospital committee would have to approve, but I see no problem. I wondered what you felt about that?'

Susy's heart was racing, her mind leaping forward. Could she do it? Even after her small steps towards renewed confidence, could she take responsibility for a children's ward? She knew her father would not rush her for an answer, so she said quietly, 'It's rather a surprise, Dad, a gratifying one at that, but let me have a little time. Not that I don't appreciate what you're offering, but I can't take on something that I may not be able to carry through.'

Her father smiled. 'My dear, you're our daughter, and your mother and I believe in you and your abilities implicitly, but we wouldn't want to put you at risk, myself either, for that matter. If I didn't think you were more than capable of doing the job I wouldn't have put this to you. There's only one thing I ask, and that is you let me know when you can.'

Later that evening before going up to bed, Susy went to her father's study where he sat dealing with overdue administration for which he could never find enough time at the hospital. He looked up with a smile. 'Come in, Susy, sit down. I suppose you're worrying about the job now?' he said with a slight frown.

'Not quite in the way you think,' Susy said guardedly, 'but I wondered what Ross might say about your offer to me.'

As she spoke, she thought how futile an obstacle it sounded. Her father obviously felt the same, as he said in some surprise, 'Ross? Why should he be a main factor in your decision? In any case, surely he'll benefit? He's off to Belfast tomorrow, but naturally I shall tell him as soon as he's back.'

'Yes, I suppose so,' she murmured, wishing she hadn't mentioned her thoughts at all. If her father felt she was able to take on the job, surely he was the one to judge?

'Cheer up, darling. Something I nearly forgot to tell you: we've decided that young Robin will be fit enough for discharge shortly. He's made a very good recovery, you know.'

She smiled happily. 'I was hoping to hear that soon, Dad, although Robin doesn't seem too eager to go.'

'That's because you're around, but he'll soon drop back into his normal routine, especially when you resume those special outings you take him on that he loves so much.'

As she got ready for bed, of all the things she had to think about suddenly, anxiety as to how Robin would settle down again once he returned to the home was uppermost in her mind. But on second thoughts she allowed herself to remember the kiss. It had only served to stir up the fires of attraction for Ross, and that was something she had to keep totally hidden.

CHAPTER SIX

ROBIN was discharged from the hospital on the day Ross and Marc returned from their brief trip to Belfast. Great excitement was rife in the children's ward, and as usual small presents and a special cake had been prepared for the homegoer.

Robin was wheeled into the orthopaedic ward after they'd held a little ceremony for him on Medical, and it was as they were coming to the finale of the excitable celebrations, and Robin was waiting to be taken home in the hospital mini-bus, that the two doctors walked in.

'Well,' Ross beamed. 'It seems we're just in time!' He forced a large frown at the boy. 'Let's see, where is it you're going this afternoon, Robin?'

Robin laughed delightedly. 'You know! I'm going home!'

Marc joined in. 'Is that right, children?'

'Yes!' came the shouts from all directions.

Marc grinned, fishing a huge parcel of Smarties from his holdall. 'Well, isn't that the luckiest thing I just happened to have these? You share them out with your friends, Robin, and if there's any left over take them home with you.'

Robin seized upon such an opportunity. 'Thank you. I'll have to save some 'cos Susy and Aunty Dorothy must share as well.'

Just then someone called Ross to the phone as he smiled. 'That's great, Robin. See you in a day or two!'

'Bye, Robin; look after yourself, now!' Marc added later, after glancing at his watch.

After being promised that she would try and visit

him next day, Robin left rather tearfully, Susy thought, but she put it down to over-excitement, and began to settle the high-spirited children into a semblance of calm before their evening meal. It was while she was at the drugs cupboard stacking away a delivery that she overheard Ross asking where she was. He came into the office, his face rather withdrawn and tense, and this did not seem quite the time to ask if things had gone well in Belfast.

'Miss Frenais.' The formality did not bode too well either, she thought, as he said brusquely, 'Can I see you in my office in about ten minutes, please?'

He left without giving her the chance to say yes or no, and she could only think that Miss Aldridge had registered a complaint. But when she went to his office by Reception, she couldn't have been more wrong.

'Come in, Susy, I won't keep you; it's probably your homegoing time now anyway,' he remarked brusquely. He was leaning against the front of his desk, long legs crossed at the ankles. 'The phone call I had earlier, when Robin was leaving, was from your father, who was unsure if I was back or not. However, he tells me that he's suggesting you apply for the staff nurse vacancy here.'

'Yes, that's right. I haven't yet given him an answer.'

'Susy——' He glanced down at his shoes then back at her. 'If you consider this post, are you sure it wouldn't still place too great a burden upon you? After all, our admission numbers could well be twice what they are at present, and it will be hard work, you know.'

'Obviously, Ross, I need to think these points over, of course, but I can't give any guarantees.'

'No, I understand that, but at this stage I wouldn't want you to undermine your newly found confidence, which it's clear you now have, but permanent employment may take a greater toll.'

While he spoke she wondered about the motive behind his words. He seemed to be trying to dissuade her. Her thoughts tumbled out recklessly. 'Is it that you don't think I'm capable of taking it on, Ross, or that you have someone else in mind?'

He looked slightly rattled. 'I would say that at present you are entirely suitable and capable, but it's more the long-term I was thinking of. As for anyone else, I imagine the committee would want to see two or three other candidates, but that need not be a problem,' he said tersely.

'Thank you, Ross. I'll bear our conversation in mind,' she said coolly, wishing she knew exactly what it was that made her think he had not taken too kindly to the idea of her being on the staff. 'Is there anything else?' she asked, turning to the door.

He straightened up from the desk, impatient with his own thoughts, his mind still latching on to the apparent closeness between Marc and Susy. Although he knew Marc had adored his wife, Marc could perhaps by now be quite susceptible to someone who had been a good friend. Ross knew also that Susy had sensed his lack of enthusiasm for her to work on the staff. He couldn't tell her, of course, but something in his subconscious kicked against his witnessing Marc's unfolding love-affair with her. As well as that, he was damned annoyed that Ian had asked her about taking the job without first consulting him; he was supposed to be designate in charge of the unit and had a right to a say in the running of it. More importantly, was his old enemy, nepotism, raising its ugly head again?

Now, as he looked at the perplexed expression on Susy's face, he felt like a heel. He had no idea what the hell was wrong with him. Ever since the girl had arrived he had wanted to get to know her better; wanted to understand what it was that seemed to be eating away at the happiness she should be finding. A broken engagement wasn't the end of the world, was it? She seemed to know her stuff as far as work was concerned but — he was back on the merry-go-round of his thoughts again — he had to admit it was Marc with whom she was at her most relaxed. He pushed back a thick lock of hair from his forehead, making a subconscious note that it was time he went to the hairdresser.

He had taken his time answering Susy. 'Um. . .oh, no, nothing more, Susy, thank you, except that I don't need to tell you we'll expect you to join the official party once the opening ceremony of the unit is over. As far as I know, there's to be a cocktail party at the Atlantic. You know the hotel, the one overlooking St Quen's Bay.' He had his hand on the door-handle.

'Quite a plush place. Thanks, I'll look forward to it.' As he opened the door, she glanced up at him and a shaft of sunlight flooded the hall outside, bringing the vague thought to him that those cool, intelligent brown eyes sometimes shone like dappled light on water. The observation, and her smile, distracted him momentarily.

'Sorry I've kept you so long; we'll talk again later, no doubt.'

He watched her slender, graceful figure walk across to the lift, and slowly closed the office door. He endeavoured to force his mind back to more mundane things, instead of which a drift of perfume lingered about his desk, fragantly delicate, until with an exasperated growl he jumped up and pushed another window wide open.

Driving home, Susy still pondered on her conviction that Ross was not wholly in agreement with her taking the job, and more and more, as she drew near Rosebriar Cottage, it was that very thing that was beginning to force her to the conclusion she jolly well *would* apply and Ross Beaumaris, for whatever reason, would sooner or later have to explain his prejudices.

But doubt almost immediately assailed her, that she
might come to regret such a decision made in the heat
of the moment.

She and Julia went out to a wine-bar that evening,
and Susy was glad to drop her present problem into
her friend's lap. 'When Ross first knew my way of
thinking about re-starting a job, he seemed completely
understanding and was all for me going back to work
as soon as I felt like it,' she concluded with a puzzled
frown. 'Now things seem totally different.'

Julia sipped her wine thoughtfully. 'But you think
the idea of you working at the unit has changed his
mind?'

'Well, it could be taken like that, but I'm really not
sure.'

The two friends stared gloomily at each other until
Julia said with a grin, 'We're probably barking up the
wrong tree anyway.'

'Could be, I suppose,' Susy agreed.

'What about this Marc Adjani you mentioned on the
phone the other day? We seem to have so much to
catch up on, but you must tell me about him.'

Susy told her how they'd met and the coincidence of
meeting up again. 'He took me out to dinner the other
night; it was great being able to talk to him about
Belfast as he'd actually worked there, if only briefly.
His wife and baby died in childbirth when they were
first married so he was wonderfully understanding
about Patrick.' Susy sighed, gazing at her ringless hand.
'It was terrific talking to someone who had been
through it all. Quite honestly, Julia, it was better than
a counselling session.'

'I can understand that, seeing that he knew Belfast
in the way that you do.'

'Yes, it sort of makes our friendship quite special.
Anyway, he's determined we shan't lose touch; I'll no
doubt be seeing him again some time soon.'

Julia looked long and hard at her friend. 'Really? You did say he's a lot older than you, didn't you?'

Susy gave her a penetrating stare. 'It's nothing like that! We really are good friends, Julia; we have in common all the awful things that have wrecked both our lives.'

'Yeah, I see what you mean,' she said slowly. 'You don't suppose this would have anything to do with Ross and his odd behaviour?'

'Heavens, no! Why should it? They're very good friends and it should make no difference to that.'

'Mmm, I just wondered.' Julia ordered two more glasses of wine. 'How's young Robin, by the way? I knew he'd gone back to the home; I presume he's OK?'

'He's recovered, yes, but I think it's going to take him a little time to settle down at the home. I was on the phone to Matron last night and she said he seems somewhat withdrawn again, as he was in the beginning. I suppose he's missing the children at the hospital.'

'And you, and Ross,' Julia said with a smile.

'That, too, perhaps. I tried hard not to give the little lad any preferential treatment while he was on the ward, but it was awfully hard; he's such a lovable child.'

'He still has his special friend, Sandra, has he?'

'Yes, although Matron said even she has failed to make much of a breakthrough with him so far. She said I can take him out tomorrow afternoon and perhaps I'll get a better idea then. I suppose she was right in holding him back at the home for a short while to get acclimatised once more.'

They talked on in general until Julia brought the conversation round to Ross again. 'I suppose you've never met Ross's ex?'.

'No, though he told me about her, or at least how the divorce came about. His wife certainly sounded forgettable. What a selfish existence she seemed to lead.'

'Too right. I've always felt rather sorry for Ross, although I don't think he's short of women-friends. There's one or two females at the hospital who have joined the chase — one in particular, Rebecca Cohen. Do you know, I've seen her watch him walk out of his office while she conceals herself in an appropriate doorway and when he walks past she strolls out, barging into him accidentally on purpose?'

'Wow! Full marks to her for trying!'

'I wouldn't run after a man like that, however crazy I was about him.'

'What would you do, then?'

'I'd find out what sort of sport he played, or favourite hobby he had, then do the same, only better! He'd notice you all right then! As I think I mentioned, I did that with John, and it worked!'

'Does she know that Ross goes sailing in his spare time? Although I can't imagine Rebecca competing at the risk of getting her hair rearranged!'

Julia giggled. 'Aren't we catty? As a matter of fact I've heard about the sailing, and I think he probably resorted to it in the first place to get over to France and avoid Miriam's hobby of spending Daddy's money!'

'Could be!'

The following day Susy had the afternoon off. She went to the home and collected Robin, his little face glowing as she packed him into the front passenger seat of the car and put his chair in the boot. It had been raining that morning and the sky was leaden with cloud and not at all promising. As they set off she said, 'How would you like to come back to my house straight away, Robin, instead of going down to the beach?

Aunty Dorothy's out, but you won't mind that, will you?'

She was surprised how readily he agreed. 'No, I don't mind, Susy, then I can sit next to you all the time.'

She glanced at him anxiously. Since leaving the hospital he seemed less confident, as if the stubborn determination in him was gradually waning. When they got home they sat on the patio, then watched a cartoon film, did a jigsaw puzzle, and she was reading one of his favourite stories to him when she glanced up to see tears in his eyes.

Swiftly she put the book aside and knelt down beside his wheelchair, taking him in her arms, his sturdy little body trembling as she asked what was wrong. Genuine sobs mangled the words in his throat, and it was a few minutes before Susy was able to make sense from the garbled sentences. 'I don't want to be 'dopted, Susy. I want to stay at the home.'

'But, darling, nothing's been said to you about being adopted, has it?' She fetched some tissues and mopped his face, the tear-stained features hot as he nodded miserably.

'Yes, now I'm better, soon I'll leave the home and be 'dopted.'

'Matron hasn't said anything to you about this at the home since you left the hospital?' Susy said, frowning.

'No, but Sandra told me she was going away to a new mummy and daddy soon if they like her.'

Susy brushed back the dark curls. 'Look, sweetheart, you've been worrying over nothing. All these things take a very long time to arrange, and I know that Matron wouldn't do any of them until she tells you all about it. She'll also tell Dr Ross.'

'And you?' he added, a small hiccup of a sob catching at his breath.

'And me,' Susy said, with more certainty than she

felt. 'Look, Robin, promise you're not going to worry
abut this any more. I'll have a talk with them at the
home about this, and remember, just because Sandra
might be going away, it doesn't necessarily mean that
you are as well.'

Robin was looking slightly more cheerful. 'Sandra
doesn't want to go unless she can take me with her.
She told me so.'

'Well, darling, we'll see what happens; don't trouble
your head about it now. Tell you what, let's go to the
kitchen and find our tea. I *think* there's some of your
favourite banana sandwiches today!'

'Chocolate sponge cake, too?'

They searched in the kitchen. 'It's our lucky day,
Robin, here's the sponge cake! I'll leave the fridge
door open and you can lift out the sandwiches!'

By the time Susy returned Robin to the home, he
seemed to have revived considerably and Susy made
sure she obtained some reassurance from Matron
before she left. Now she drove through the grounds
and back down towards the gates in a much relieved
state of mind. A car was turning into the drive, and to
her surprise she saw it was Ross. He immediately
moved over towards the grass verge and ran his window
down, calling, 'Hello!' Have you had Robin this
afternoon?'

'Yes, I've just taken him back, as a matter of fact.'

'In that case I won't go in now; I'm rather too late,
anyway.'

'That's a pity; I'm sure he'd like to see you.'

'No, I'd rather leave it until tomorrow; Friday's
usually the day I go for checking.'

'Ross, I'm a bit concerned about him, though. . .'

Another car had entered the drive. Ross began to
move his vehicle, calling, 'I'll just park this out of the
way. Hang on a minute.'

He came back and sat in her passenger seat, leaving the door open. 'Now, what was this about the boy?'

She repeated her thoughts. 'He still seems very tearful; it seems such a shame after he'd been settling in so well before he went into the hospital.'

'What do you think caused it?'

She glanced at her wristwatch. 'Well, perhaps I'll leave telling you until tomorrow. I've just remembered Mum and Dad are going out tonight and want to eat at six.'

'Well, I've an idea John Fornet is dragging me off to a badminton knock-about tonight; supposing I call in to your place on the way back?'

'Um. . . I. . .' she stuttered, trying not to appear too eager.

He must have taken it the wrong way, for his smile faded. 'No problem, of course,' he said curtly. 'If you're doing something else we can talk about it tomorrow.'

She found her tongue, his sudden small burst of enthusiasm having cast its usual spell, her heart already thumping out its jungle beat. 'Oh, no,' she said, as leisurely as she could. ' I just thought if you'd been playing badminton you wouldn't want to go to the trouble of coming to my place.'

He smiled again, noticing the charming rose colour that suffused her cheeks; it must be to do with some sort of embarrassement that her feelings for Robin were no longer private. 'It'll be no trouble at all, Susy. I'll be there some time after eight.'

Over the evening meal at home she told her parents about Robin, and that Ross was calling in to discuss it.

'That's a good thing, Susy,' her father said. 'We'll all have to get together about the boy sooner or later, I'm thinking.'

When her parents had gone, Susy stacked the dinner things into the dishwasher and switched it on, then went upstairs to her room. Firstly she read a letter from her brother which she skimmed through lightly and put aside to be savoured later; next she opened her wardrobe door, wondering what to wear that evening, but immediately reminded herself that it was not a date as such, merely an extension of work that could be dicussed without interruption. She pulled on a pair of blue jeans and a floppy shirt embroidered down the front with rather dizzy patterns in paintbox colours, and slipped her feet into flat sandals. 'Never let it be said that I'm trying to seduce our Dr Beaumaris in this gear,' she murmured to her reflection, while brushing down her hair from its restricting pins. 'He wouldn't look twice at me in this shirt. I wonder why I bought it?'

Her subconscious gave her the answer. Since Patrick's death she'd bought things she didn't want; gone to places she didn't like, and, to keep her emotions intact, said things she didn't mean. With a small sigh she went downstairs and sat on the patio, flipping through a magazine. Her mind roamed; nothing seemed to make much sense that evening. Deep down she was thinking of her dinner date with Marc on the coming Sunday. For some reason she felt mildly uncomfortable about it. She hoped he wasn't seeing anything long-term in their friendship. It was just one or two things he'd said the last time they spoke to each other that made her wonder.

A ring at the doorbell banished these thoughts as, lightly, she ran through the house and opened the door to see. . . Marc standing grinning happily at her!

'Hi, Susy! Hope this isn't inconvenient. I just happened to be in the locality and thought I'd drop in for a chat, if that's OK?'

She gulped back. . .disappointment?

'Sure, Marc! No, it's OK; do come in.'

'Great! I thought you looked a bit surprised there for a moment.'

'No, actually Ross had said he might call in later to discuss work, but that's another thing altogether!'

'Well, I wouldn't dream of intruding upon that!'

They sat on the patio, Marc relaxed and genial as ever. 'How are things, Susy?'

For a while they talked of things in general, of people they knew, until he said with a smile, 'I haven't had a chance to tell you of our trip to Belfast yet. Everyone back there sends love and best wishes. They were just as surprised as I was to know that we'd met up. From all accounts they still miss you, Susy, and hope you'll go back to see them some day.'

A lump rose in her throat. 'I will, Marc, eventually. The very thought of the place still chokes me up, I'm afraid.'

He placed a comforting hand over hers. 'Susy, my dear, that sort of reaction isn't going to do anything but good, you know, because of the fact that it took so long for you to give way to your grief when your troubles started. I know myself it seemed the right thing to do, to keep that stiff upper lip and not allow others to see how you were coping. In certain circles, it's something we're taught to do. Grief has to be hidden; we mustn't reveal our feelings in public, so we bottle it up. Grief cannot be seen, and people tend to forget that months later it's still there like a terrible amputation, and everyone thinks you no longer need their consolation, which is just not true. It affects everything we do. A demanding job, most of all.'

She smiled gratefully. 'Marc, I need to be reminded of that. Not that others haven't said similar things, but knowing you yourself have actually experienced it in the same way makes all the difference. You too know all these small sufferings one tries to hide, like feeling so alone in a crowded street or room.'

'Believe me, Susy, it will pass.' He removed his hand from hers as if having forgotten it was there. She knew what all that was about too, the desperate longing to touch and be touched; to be loved in so many small, unobtrusive ways, when so much had been taken for granted. 'I'm sure you're right, Marc; it won't be for the want of trying from now on.'

He smiled, open admiration for her on his face. 'You know, you're quite a girl, Susy. You're going to come right through this whole thing with flying colours, and you'll be better than ever, I just know it.'

'Well, I suppose I'm taking a few steps in the right direction. Sorry, Marc—what about a drink?'

He stood up. 'Let me get them. What would you like?'

She watched him cross to the drinks trolley, looking at his tough, athletic body, those heavy shoulders, his thick silvered hair and deep transatlantic tan. Why had his own life taken such a cruel turn? He handed Susy her drink with a gentle smile, compassion and understanding in everything he did. She must have been crazy earlier even to think that his comments had hinted at a future that might include her. He was one of those strong-minded characters who loved only once in a lifetime. He sat down, placing his drink on a small table, practically taking the thoughts from her head.

'You know, Susy, there are times when you show exactly the same fortitude as my wife when she was a medical student. Slap in the middle of her course her beloved father died, committed suicide after his firm collapsed around his ears. There was no money and she wouldn't accept help from anyone. She paid her way by taking numerous temporary jobs wherever she could. She sure fought back, and won. I just know you'll do the same.'

'As it happens, that could just be a possibility,' she said quietly, gazing into her glass. 'Dad has asked me if I'd like to apply for the job of staff nurse in the new peds unit.'

Marc beamed. 'That's terrific, hon! Why so solemn?'

'Well, for one thing I haven't yet given Dad an answer, and for another I don't think Ross wholly approves.'

'Doesn't approve!' Marc exclaimed. 'How come?'

'When he returned from Belfast, Dad told him, and he just seemed sort of disgruntled. Asked me if I'd given it enough thought and all that stuff—if I didn't think the permanency of the job might be too much for me. I simply gained the impression that he just didn't want me to take it for reasons best known to himself.'

'Does your father know this?'

'I did just suggest that Ross might not be too keen about the offer being made without consulting him, but that didn't seem to cut any ice with Dad.'

'And you've still to give a reply?'

'Yes, but it can wait another day or two.'

'Well, I know it's none of my business, but if you feel up to it I wouldn't turn it down lightly.'

'I feel very much that way myself.'

'No doubt you'll tell me how things went. Before I forget, how's the little boy who was discharged back to the home?'

'Robin? He's not too bad.'

'That doesn't sound too good!'

'I'm just a bit worried about him, Marc. He's not settling down happily; he's been quite tearful, in fact, since he got back. He's a sensitive child and he's heard about adoption and all it entails. I think it's completely tilted what was becoming his safe little world.'

'Gee, that's tough. Well, let's hope it can be sorted out.'

'That's one of the things I want to talk to Ross about tonight if he comes.'

He glanced at his watch and stood up. 'Yep, I ought

to be moving myself. I have some notes to write up for a lecture I'm giving on the mainland in a couple of days. I sure wish I could stay on longer, Susy, but there's so much I want to do while I'm over here. Oh, yes, and another thing. I've arranged for ten youngsters from Belfast to be brought out to San Francisco in the coming fall. Boy, are they excited! But you can bet we'll give them a time they'll never forget!'

When Marc left, she closed the door thoughtfully, ever mindful of the ability he possessed to make her feel so much better. As she closed the door, she thought she had heard a second car on the drive, but decided she must have been mistaken.

CHAPTER SEVEN

Ross drove along Rosebriar Lane, and pulled into the grass verge to allow an approaching vehicle to pass, then realised it was Marc in his hired car.

Marc called through the open window, 'Hi, Ross, she's expecting you!'

Ross waved as the other car carried on. He frowned, switching off his engine impatiently, needing time to think. Was there something between Marc and Susy based on their first meeting in Belfast? He was irritated with himself that he should even think such a thing or that it would worry him, and yet it did. Maybe it was the thought that he would have staked his life on Marc's complete and utter devotion to his dead wife, and what he felt was a suggestion of disillusionment. But surely that was wrong? Marc. . .everyone deserved another chance of happiness, and wouldn't it be more to the point if he were truthful and admitted it was because he also would like to get to know Susy? Really know her. He was worried too that she could be drawn to the older man on the rebound, and should that be the case she might well be headed for more despair than ever if Marc had no intentions along those lines and Susy had misread the signs.

He switched on the ignition suddenly, moving back on to the road towards Rosebriar Cottage, his thoughts going from one thing to another. The idea of her working in the unit was also something else he had been totally unprepared for. Although Ian had now told him, Ross considered it quite wrong that Ian should have mentioned it to Susy before himself. The whole thing rankled badly, and should he happen to see Ian that evening he'd damned well tell him so.

When Susy opened the front door most of his resentment vanished. She looked quite delectable in jeans with a colourful top, the fresh but casual appearance lighting up her entire face. In different circumstances he would have swept her off her feet and swung her round before kissing those Botticelli lips, he thought fancifully.

'Hi, Ross. Come in!' she invited, thinking that for a man who had just played a hard game with John Fornet he looked remarkably cool and fit. 'You've only just missed Marc; he called in unexpectedly.'

'I thought so just now. I didn't recognise the car until he called out as he went past. I hope two members of staff in one evening isn't too much?

'The more the merrier! Mum and Dad have gone off to one of their bridge parties, as a matter of fact. They'll be hours yet, so it was going to be a long evening, anyway.'

As he stepped into the hall, Bill and Ben rushed up to him. She closed the door while he returned the dogs' welcome. He unzipped the top of his red and black tracksuit, revealing a black cotton top that did little to conceal his well-developed pectoral muscles, enhancing his attractiveness even more. Normally she had only seen him in formal dress, and now as he pushed a hand through a dark swath of hair, smiling at her in a drowsy, sensuous way, remarking upon the dogs, she needed to remind herself that after a day's work followed by badminton anyone would have an air of languorous sleepiness.

Talking as they walked out to the patio, Susy was still conscious of the same old telltale tingle skittering along her spine, as if her body had immediately set up its own form of Morse Code. She hardly needed to be prompted to get the message. This man seemed to possess the sort of magnetism that nudged her similar passion for the English master back to life, something that by now should have been well and truly over; it was, but seemingly the signals remained. And, having admitted as much, she now had to try and act as the outwardly sophisticated person she liked to think she was.

Ross had strolled across to the terraced area, gazing beyond the garden to the sea as it lay glimmering in the setting sun. She stood at his side and they watched a cruise ship slide silently along the ruler-straight horizon. 'This view is quite beautiful, you know,' he murmured admiringly, turning to her, thinking how apt his words were in more ways than one.

'Yes, we love it. I've realised how much I missed the island while I was away.' She hoped her voice sounded normal; it was as if she was still acting the part of herself as the gauche sixteen-year-old, tongue-tied, unsure. Being in such close proximity to Ross and feeling his eyes holding hers brought on a pounding in her ears, her blood was racing; she could hardly tear her eyes from that dark, penetrating gaze.

Ross seemed to be seeing her for the first time. The same fragrance of her perfume drifted between them. The low-cut neck opening of the top she wore gave a tantalising glimpse of full, rounded breasts. She seemed both innocent and seductive, and he was powerless to draw his eyes from her.

The telephone resolved the situation. Susy emerged as if from a dream. 'Excuse me, Ross,' she murmured. 'Do. . .do sit down.' She crossed the patio to the phone extension, her heart still beating madly, her voice vibrating as she spoke.

Ross strolled out again to the terrace below the patio, having to clear his chaotic thoughts. Susy Frenais, who had at first meeting seemed so unapproachable in every way, cloaked as she was with her own secret unhappiness, now so informally dressed and moving with such feline grace, sensual yet totally unselfconscious, was a revelation. Even as she spoke to one of her mother's friends', her voice held a more light-hearted, humorous quality that revealed yet another facet of her personality. A moment ago his heart had hammered at her closeness, a physical reaction he had not needed to worry about for some time. Was it because she seemed so elusive, an enigma, that made her all the more desirable, or, even less honourably, was it because his best friend was showing an interest? Furthermore, there was this mystique about her that was so very personal and private. She had not taken him into her confidence as no doubt she had Marc. The thought brought on an unexpected pang of jealousy which he swiftly quelled.

She had replaced the receiver and crossed over to the drinks trolley as he strolled back into the patio. 'Sorry about that, Ross. What will you have?'

He smiled with a shake of the head. 'Not for me, thanks, Susy, really.'

'Coffee, perhaps?'

'Please, I'd love it. I'll come out to the kitchen with you.'

'Do.' She grinned. 'It's where a good many of our friends are comfortable in this house!'

He watched her spoon beans into the coffee grinder, transfer the coffee to the cafetière, plug in the kettle and set a tray for two.

They talked then of nothing in particular, as if quite suddenly it was necessary to fill the small gaps of silence such as the one that had fallen between them before the phone rang. He was glad of the respite to allow his mind to clear, reminding him yet again that there was still a lot about her that he didn't know, but that sooner or later he had to find out. After all, if she did take the job in his unit, it might be imperative to

know. The tentative feelers he'd put forward to Marc
about it had not resulted in answers, for Marc had not
been forthcoming, and Ross did not want his words to
be misunderstood as an intrusion into Marc and Susy's
friendship, which had obviously been forged under
great stress.

She had piled everything on to the tray and he
carried it back to the patio. Dusk had smudged the
room with shadow now, and she switched on two large
table lamps that cast soft discs of gold as they sat down
with a long, low coffee-table between them. Susy
poured, handing him a cup, as he said suddenly, 'Now,
what was this you wanted to say about Robin, Susy?
You were quite concerned earlier.'

She leaned back on the cushions, allowing her drink
to cool, as well as her mind, as she said, 'I am still.'
She gave him the details that had led up to her own
discovery of Robin's misery, continuing, 'The whole
thing is so worrying considering the strides he had
made since first going to the home.'

'So you think it might have been sparked off by
young Sandra's comment?'

'Well, not entirely. Nevertheless, that perhaps, as
well as snippets the child had picked up for himself on
the adoption thing, and which maybe had been in the
back of his mind until he went to the hospital, when a
careless remark might well have set him thinking again
and unsettled him quite badly. Added to that, his other
friends, chatter about the same thing and how they are
going to stay with a "new" mum and dad. Meanwhile
Robin had bottled up all this until he felt able to tell
me.'

'He seems very fond of you, Susy. Are you sure it's
wise?' he asked gently.

She felt a twinge of conscience, knowing even before
the child that they needed each other in their loneliness. 'Well, I could be to blame, I suppose, Ross. He's

such a sweet child, we get on so well together and I can't bear the thought of him being unhappy.'

'Yes, of course I understand that, Susy, but there are many other children just as appealing, and you, of all people in the sort of job we do, know how hard it is not to love these youngsters as individuals. It's impossible not to draw a line somewhere, and as adults it's up to us to enforce that.' He saw the mist of tears in her eyes and hated himself for being so blunt.

'I know you're right, Ross,' she said quietly, 'but every now and again one child seems to claim the heart. And the chemistry, if it can be called that, creates an immediate bond.'

'You mean rather as it is when two people. . .fall in love at first sight, only a different sort of love?'

She had the feeling he had purposely veered the conversation around, and sipped her coffee, glancing away as she settled the cup back in the saucer. 'Well, I suppose you could say that. I imagine it's just the right balance between two opposing age groups.'

He did not intend allowing the subject to rest there. 'So, Robin aside for the moment, do I gather that you've never fallen in love at first sight?'

'I. . . I'm not sure.' She grinned, adding flippantly, 'And if I had I don't think I'd talk about it too much!'

'Fascinating thought, though, isn't it? Just imagine, you could meet someone at Heathrow, hands touch for some reason, and — boom! — there it is again, and with a perfect stranger, no less!'

Her subconscious was bang on cue when she heard herself saying with slight changes, 'As a matter of fact I did have a friend to whom it happened; her mother told her — this was when we were at school — that it could either be a passing sexual encounter, or the love of a lifetime.'

Ross smiled. 'And what did it turn out to be for

your—um—friend?' His eyes twinkled, looking very knowing.

It was obvious he didn't believe her, but she ploughed on. 'Well. . .not very happily, I'm afraid. It was just a turn-on and that was all. But it did take her months to get over it and she never forgot the experience.'

'And it hasn't ever happened to you again since?'

'I——' She broke off, blushing furiously. 'Ross! I didn't say it was me, I said it was a schoolfriend of mine, if you remember.'

'I see.' He laughed, putting up a hand as if to fend off her wrath. 'I'll believe you! But why so coy? You know, there's quite a lot I have to learn about you yet.'

'Is there? Well, I don't go around with my heart on my sleeve.'

He touched her face with his hand, almost a reflex action, before dropping it again. 'Now don't go all serious on me! Wearing your heart on your sleeve is quite different from what we were talking about.'

The fleeting brush with his fingers against her cheek had quite thrown her. 'R-Ross,' she stammered,' this conversation has come a long way from Robin and his problems.'

'I know. But do you realise I've hardly had a chance to really talk to you, to get to know what goes on beneath that cool, and sometimes remote, exterior? I think, Susy, there's quite a lot you haven't told me about your time in Belfast. Something that prevents you from being the open, warm-hearted, fun-loving girl I think you are.'

'The engagement, Ross, it takes time——'

He broke in, 'I know, but forgive me—it must have been a wrench, yes, but it's not. . .not like someone . . .dying, for instance. The engagement might have turned out to be a mistake, anyway.'

Her heart had given a great lurch at his words, words

that sliced into her heart and sent a spurt of anger
through her. 'I'm sorry, Ross, that's maybe how you
see it, but I don't! There's something else I want to
say, too. I have made up my mind to apply for the job
in the unit, and if I were offered it just tell me
something. Am I going to be grilled by you to supply
all my innermost thoughts on my private life? Because
if so I'll forget the whole thing!' She banged down her
coffee-cup and stood up, her entire body shaking as
she stamped out to the terrace, staring out across the
water but not seeing it.

A soft footfall sounded behind her. Two firm hands
turned her round to face him. Through a blur of tears
she looked at him, arms wrapped tight across her
breasts as if she were cold. He said nothing, but
carefully, silently, loosed her arms and placed them at
her sides, then cupped her face between his two hands.

'Susy, my apologies. I had no intention of hurting
your feelings, or upsetting you; it was thoughtless of
me.' His hands slipped down to her shoulders. 'At first
we were just exchanging light-hearted banter between
us, and I didn't realise how quickly it had turned to
something more serious. Believe me, if you applied for
the job, I wouldn't intrude upon your private life. It's
just that I know you've come through a big trauma and
so often it helps to talk about it. OK, I know you find
it easier to talk to Marc—he knows more about your
time in Belfast than I do; nevertheless, I have your
interests at heart, and if you do apply for the job—and
get it—I would want to know that you were able to
give your full potential to the work without the burden
of personal worries which——'

'Could make me more of a hindrance on your staff,
is that it?' she interrupted explosively, eyes flashing,
the gold flecks sparking with anger. Her breasts heaved
with her ragged breathing, and she tried to move from
him, unsuccessfully. 'You, Ross Beaumaris, have

simply no idea of my private concerns, and why should you?' she said with a derisive laugh. 'But for the purpose of the new job, I know that I have recovered and am well able to take it on, so your anxieties are groundless! Shall I tell you what really gets me?' she demanded.

He said nothing, only continued to hold her in his manacled grip, while she answered her own question.

'Right, I will!' she gasped, racing on like an express train about to jump the lines. 'I think your ego has been dented because my father offered this job to me, and your vanity precludes your accepting the situation with dignity! All you can do now is to dig up excuses about my personal affairs which have nothing at all to do with you, or my professional life!' She tried to tug away from him, the closeness an irritation because it was necessary to tilt her head back to look him in the eye, and worst of all she could hear his heartbeats thumping away against her own.

His hold had tightened upon her even more, the dark eyes smouldered with anger, the thick strand of hair that had fallen across his forehead giving him the appearance of a man whose emotions were goading him on to perform some basic primeval act beyond his control. 'Listen to me, woman,' he grated threateningly. 'You can say what the hell you like, you can think whatever you like, but, as for my so-called vanity being a motivation for my thoughts, you couldn't be more wrong! As I see things now, I was the one at fault to confide in you about the selfishness of my ex-wife when we went out to dinner. You obviously haven't the wit, the experience or the wisdom to understand what I was trying to do in talking to you that way; your mind is about as narrow as a miser's smile. I should have realised that, too. You are just Daddy and Mummy's little girl, and it's about time you grew up!' he thundered, giving her a final shake away from him.

Shocked at his outburst, she trembled with fury at his words, and without thinking her hand came up and connected with his face in a stinging blow. Her cheeks burned as she retaliated fiercely, 'Don't you dare have the nerve to say such a thing to me ever again. I. . . I think you had better go!'

A moment of fearful silence hung like a poised sword between them, and then, as if a time bomb had exploded in the highly charged atmosphere, Ross suddenly threw back his head with a great gale of laughter. 'Oh, dear, we are getting all Victorian, aren't we? And why shouldn't we finish off this gripping drama in the time-honoured way?' he muttered sardonically, eyes as dark as night.

And before she realised what he was doing she was imprisoned once more in his arms and his lips came down hard upon hers, passionate, unrelenting and cruel — leaving her, to her chagrin, squirming to escape exactly like a Victorian maiden! But he was not allowing her to get away so lightly. With a short laugh, but still holding her against him, he let a gradual change take place in the pressure of his mouth upon hers, a gentle, more tender contact, from which he lifted his lips briefly to murmur, 'I am not apologising!'

She parted her lips to speak, but there was no chance as his lips claimed hers again, forcing them to stay apart as his tongue made contact with hers, sending the blood singing through her veins while his arms bound her like iron thongs, making her soft breasts strain against him. His hand ran caressingly through the silken fall of her hair, stroked the peach-like texture of the nape of her neck, which silently made her long for the sensation to go on forever as her entire body succumbed to these sweet new longings. Together, it seemed, they soared to a pinnacle of slowly rising frenzy, his hoarse breathing tearing at him, hers a series of small groans of delight with the onset of intimate kisses such as she had rarely experienced.

Until the sudden drone of a plane climbing high up into the sky seemed to draw them back to reality, and slowly, very slowly, they returned to earth like a final shower of stars from a brilliant firework that had rocketed high in the sky by mistake.

Bemused, breathless, Susy tried to avert her face from his, hardly able to believe what had happened, but still wondering if she really had said those things to Ross that had goaded him to such anger, and then on . . .to this. His arms fell to his sides, as she whispered huskily, 'It was my fault, Ross, I'm truly sorry.'

He pushed back his hair, his face that of a man after ending a traumatic journey. He drew her down on to the settee, taking her hands as he said calmly, 'Don't apologise, Susy. I'm the one around here who does all the apologising when it's necessary, understand?' He smiled, lifting her face gently by the chin. 'Agreed?'

She shook her head, lovely eyes still sultry yet ultra bright. 'Yes, but I. . .'

He placed a slim forefinger against her lips. 'No buts, promise?'

She nodded, admiring his hands as hers still lay in his. 'Promise.'

'Good. Let me tell you something, Susy; your. . . outburst — putting me in my place, I mean — has given me more of an insight into the real you than anything you've said since we first met, do you know that?'

She gave a rueful grin. 'I'm not sure which way to take that.'

'You will, when you think it over. There's just one more thing I want to say before I go. No one would be more delighted than me if you get this job. You have to believe me, it would be good for you all round.'

'Thank you, Ross,' she said sincerely. 'Perhaps we

should both forget the things we said to each other this evening?'

'Why should we? A few home truths now and again never hurt anyone!'

'In some respects, I suppose you're right.'

Her parents arrived at that point, and Susy went into the kitchen to reheat the coffee, and to make sure that she didn't look quite as shattered as she felt. Eventually, when Ross left, they lingered briefly at the open front door. He brushed a strand of hair back from her cheek, smiling, his mouth tilting at the corners, eyes still deep with questions as yet unanswered. 'Susy,' he said softly, 'don't forget *everything* that happened tonight, eh?'

She went to bed in a dream, sleep evading her for what seemed hours. She realised how little they'd eventually talked about Robin. How little they had talked about anything conclusive. As he had said, he knew her better for her outburst. In a strange sort of way, his kisses, both tumultous and tender, had made her feel the same about him.

Next morning the ambulance brought in two young children to be admitted. Staff Nurse Mason was in charge with two extra young student nurses to help on the ortho ward, and everything seemed to be running smoothly. Susy had gone into the office where Hilary Mason was reading through the night report. She looked up at Susy. 'Hi; it seems to have been a quiet night.' She smiled, with a look of relief.

'Hilary, about the official opening of the unit on Wednesday. Is it OK for me to have the afternoon off after the ceremony? I've been invited to the Atlantic for the cocktail party which is quite early. Five until six, I believe.'

'Yes, of course! I hope to be going myself, but by all means have the afternoon off. I shall be having an hour or so, which will be enough for me. I can change here.'

'Thanks, Hilary, you're a pal.'

'Tell you what, Susy, perhaps you'd do something for me. Instead of my presence on the doctor's round this morning, would you stand in? I'm needed elsewhere. I'm afraid.'

'Yes, sure, if that's permissible?'

'I don't see why not by now!'

Susy went off into the ward to settle the two new admissions before her father and Ross arrived for the round and to examine the newcomers. Both children — a boy aged nine, and a girl of three — were sorry victims of car accidents. The boy had a broken leg, and the girl a suspected fissure fracture of the skull.

The two men arrived just as Susy and the two students had shepherded those children who were well enough into the day playroom, and settled those left in the wards to remain as tidy as they could. 'Just for a little while please, Kevin!' she called to the mischievous child since he'd made such progress.

'Can't I get up yet, then, Susy?'

Kevin was doing so well and there seemed to be no holding him back since his neck was really beginning to straighten up, making him look quite a different child.

'You know you jolly well can, but you have to wait until the doctors have gone,' Susy said in her best schoolteacher voice.

'OK, then,' Kevin said, suitably chastened. 'When can I see Robin, please?'

Susy smoothed his daytime counterpane down. 'Kevin Stannard, you're full of awkward questions this morning, do you know that? When your mum takes you home, she'll probably do it then.'

'Can't he come and see me here?'

'If you're very good, I'll see if I can arrange it.'

Ross appeared at that moment. Her father was already in the medical ward. Her heart banged like the proverbial sledge-hammer; it was the first time since last night that she had allowed herself to think of Ross and what had happened between them. She was almost afraid to do so, wondering what her conclusions might be and how she was going to rid herself of this crazy attraction towards this man, which she knew, courtesy of her schoolfriend's mother, was merely physical infatuation, and equally unimportant for him, no doubt. All she wanted was to be able to look him in the eye when he spoke to her as he was doing now, without feeling she was floundering in a bowl of marshmallow.

'Morning, Nurse.' Ross was smiling. 'Morning, children! Now, let's see, who have we got here?'

Susy pulled back the little girl's bed curtains; her mother with her was in tears, holding the fretful child's hand, and looking even more anxious when Ross began to examine the child's head, and then read her notes. 'We'll have the X-ray equipment brought in here, I think, Nurse,' he said, putting the medical chart aside. 'Then we'll get the true picture.'

'She will be all right, won't she, Doctor?' the mother asked fearfully.

'Well, until we see the results of the X-ray, Mrs Marshall, we won't know for sure, but I'm inclined to be optimistic about Merry, you know. I'd say it may just be a question of resting here and keeping her under observation for a day or two. If so, she'll be a very lucky child.'

They moved on to the boy. The routine was much the same: examination, X-ray, and in his case a trip to the theatre later that morning for a plaster to be applied to a rather unpleasant Potts fracture. The three remaining bed patients were checked, and while Susy took prescriptions back to the office Ross went along to the playroom to see the children and judge their progress. Later he finished up in the office for coffee. 'Yes, Staff had to rush off somewhere; that's why I stood in for her this morning, Susy told him in answer to his question.

'I see. Well——' he smiled in a businesslike manner '—I'll just have a quick cup, please, Susy. Ian and I have a few points to discuss before he makes off to his consulting rooms this morning.'

When he had gone, Susy pondered upon what the nature of those talks might be. It still rankled that Ross was annoyed at her father for offering her the job before consulting him. To her it still seemed on the cards that she might yet not have the job offered her. Ross Beaumaris was a charmer of the first order. He did not mix business with pleasure. However contrite and flattering he might have been the night before, it would have no bearing on any decision made to his satisfaction, either the following day, or at any time in the future.

Working busily away sorting out the stock cupboard in the office, Susy felt at times that she really hated Ross Beaumaris, he unnerved her, unsettled her, and if by some chance she were offered the job, would he undermine her? There was just no telling how he would jump, and never in her life, despite what he said, would she forget his jibe about her being Daddy's little girl. Could he possibly be hinting that she was like his ex-wife, that she too was spoilt by a doting father and that suggesting the job to her in the first place smacked of nepotism? Oh, no, surely he couldn't have meant that? He fell out of love with his wife because she had too much money from her father. That certainly was not the case in her family, nor would she have wanted it that way. Nevertheless, she did seem to get caught up in other people's affairs almost against her will.

Yet, thank heaven, Marc still remained a confidant about Patrick, of whom she could now talk endlessly. Marc was so understanding, and his philosophy for living was one she wished she possessed herself. She

was eternally grateful to him for the way he had helped
put her loss into perspective; for that was what he had
done, and he knew how much her recovery and new
outlook upon life meant to her and always would.

Susy had been given Monday afternoon off and she
planned to go for a bathe at a small cove she knew,
where holiday-makers rarely appeared because it
entailed crossing a small channel of water by boat, and
being thoroughly certain of the tides. At her home they
had always kept a small rowing boat ever since she and
Graham had been at school, and it was moored on an
inlet of water at the bottom of the garden. Both she
and her brother had been strong swimmers and sailors
all their lives, along with their parents, and later Susy
had whiled away many a happy hour at the cove
whenever possible.

That afternoon she took fruit and a Coke with her
swimming things, and after about twenty minutes in
the water she stretched out her lithe body to the hot
sun. She had a book to read too, but her own thoughts
kept intruding as she lay on a towel in her bikini, and
eventually she gave up trying to read and tried to
unravel some of the problems disturbing her peace of
mind. It was while drowsily observing small puffs of
cotton-wool cloud drifting across the sapphire sky that
she also watched a small sailing boat hugging the
coastline, its dark blue sails like a twist of toffee paper
against the vast pale grey-blue ocean. It could easily
have been Ross alone out there gaining tranquillity of
mind from his taxing job. He seemed a man of infinite
patience.

In her somnolent state she imagined Ross stripped
to the waist, pitting his skills against the vast emptiness
of the ocean. He must be extremely strong. The warm
sun and sand, the rocking movement of the sea, lulled
her into a rather unpleasant fantasy where she had

swum out too far and he had to rescue her when she was going under for the third time. With a laugh at her crazy notions, she suddenly realised the afternoon had put her in a much calmer frame of mind, even if she did have to enter the realms of fantasy.

When she arrived home her mother was in the kitchen and seemingly surrounded by piles of ironing. Dorothy looked up with a smile, thinking how much fitter Susy was looking lately. 'Hello, dear, good swim?'

'Super, Mum, thanks.' She glanced at her mother's labours. 'Dad's not making you take in washing to pay for the holiday, I hope?' she quipped.

Dorothy giggled. 'Hope not, darling! But the news is I think we can now safely say that at last we'll be taking this holiday. They've offered us two cancelled bookings on a West Indies cruise, and your father has said yes! Hence all the domestic activity!'

'That's terrific, Mum. When are you leaving?'

'Next week, so I'm spinning.'

'Phew, I should think so. Well, I'd help out but I promised to go over and have a word with Matron this afternoon about Robin and this adoption thing that's worrying him.'

'Oh, dear, yes, poor little chap. I do so hope this blows over for him.'

Susy parked the car at the home, knowing that at present most of the children were at tea and Matron would have a few moments to herself. The older woman came out to the front hall to greet Susy and show her into the office.

'Do come in, my dear. I've asked them to bring us in some tea, then we won't be disturbed.' With magical precision a small trolley was brought in, and when Matron had poured and they had settled back in their chairs she said worriedly, 'I'm afraid there isn't a lot more I can tell you about Robin, you know.'

'Is he still as morose, Mrs Harris?'

'He's certainly not yet his old self. He was fine before he went to the hospital. I just don't understand it.'

Susy sighed. 'To some extent, it's when the children get talking together.'

Mrs Harris sighed. 'I know. That's something we can do very little about, I'm afraid.'

Together they went over all the aspects of Robin's young life, yet drew no real conclusions, but at least they promised each other to talk on a regular basis about the boy. By the time Susy left the kindly woman's presence she felt a little easier in her mind, yet the big problem still remained that if someone wished to adopt the boy and take him home for trial periods, was that going to disturb him even more?

CHAPTER EIGHT

THE cocktail party at the Atlantic on Wednesday evening had arrived at a point of mellowness when all the guests were congratulating each other on what a splendid inauguration of the paediatric unit it had turned out to be.

Ian Frenais glanced round from the small group of people to whom he was talking, including his wife, when he saw his daughter Susy appear in the doorway. 'Ah, here she is at last!'

'Hi, Mum, Dad! Traffic was awful; sorry I'm a bit late.'

'You're here now, not to worry. Come and meet everyone.' He drew her towards the group, introducing her to several people whom she had never met before, and some she had, including Ross. He was dressed in a silver-grey suit, blue and white striped shirt, and Varsity tie. Susy had to steel herself to make small talk while watching those firm lips smiling, talking to friends and colleagues, yet at the same time remembering his kisses that had set her on fire.

Hurriedly she joined the throng of familiar faces, really enjoying the sort of event she would have deplored a few months ago.

Nevertheless, she was quite relieved on finding Marc at her side; he was smiling at her, taking her elbow. 'Susy, it's only seven-thirty. What about us getting away from here and having dinner somewhere else — what do you say?'

'That sounds great to me, Marc.' She had just glimpsed Ross with Rebecca. 'I'll just go and say a few farewells.'

When she was ready they walked out to the foyer at the same moment that Ross and Rebecca appeared, she hanging on his arm possessively. Ross beamed. 'Marc! Susy! We were looking for you. How about joining us for dinner away from the familiar faces?'

Marc was enthusiastic. 'What do you think, girls?'

They both agreed, and all four headed for the taxi Ross had already ordered; as they drove away Susy was still piqued at the way Rebecca was clinging to Ross, but at the same time reprimanded herself that it was nothing at all to do with her.

The restaurant they went to was on the quieter side of the island, and well-known for its cuisine. In the main dining area a pianist was established at a white grand piano and played quietly and pleasantly enough to enable both conversation at the tables, and for the occasional dancers to hear each other. Susy's spirits had not been exactly buoyant. An evening with Marc alone might have been less unsettling. His words of wisdom, too, were always like balm to her troubled mind. She hardly liked to think of the time when he would soon be on the other side of the Atlantic.

Over dinner there was, nevertheless, enough to talk about. Rebecca was staring absently at a couple dancing, and said, appearing bored suddenly, 'Well, what about trying that apology for a dance-floor, Ross?'

Several people had the same idea as the evening lengthened. Marc danced with Susy, eager to know if she was enjoying herself.

'Great, thanks, Marc; it's a really swish place.'

'I think so, too. Is Rebecca someone special in Ross's life, do you know?' he asked suddenly, when they squeezed past Ross and Rebecca who looked as if they were bonded together.

'I honestly don't know, Marc.'

He grinned. 'There's only one way to find out, then!'

When Marc and Rebecca danced away, Ross held out a hand to Susy. 'Shall we?'

He put his arms around her just as the lights were lowered even more, and by now the piano was joined by drums and a saxophone playing a dreamy rendition of a Nat King Cole number, 'Smoke Gets in Your Eyes'. It was hardly possible to move at all, except that Susy didn't particularly want to, even though she had no option, and Ross was looking down at her with a speculative frown between his brows. 'I don't think I've ever seen you wear black before, Susy, strapless and fitting like a glove. Just what the doctor ordered, I'd say!'

'Ah, but which one?' She grinned cheekily, suddenly feeling she was walking on air, though hardly moving might be more accurate. 'I've come to the conclusion that you, Dr Beaumaris are an outrageous flirt!'

'Well, I never; how could you work that out, Susy? I'm totally dedicated to my work!'

'That's no excuse, and besides, I'm talking out of work hours!'

He rested his lips against her forehead. 'Mmm, your perfume's divine; what is it?'

She giggled. 'That's just what I mean! I overheard you saying exactly that to Rebecca when Marc and I danced past you a minute ago.'

His eyes held hers with devilment. 'Susy Frenais, believe me, I was doing it simply to make you jealous!'

'Well, isn't that funny? I was whispering sweet nothings into Marc's ear to make you jealous!'

'In that case, you know what we'll have to do, don't you?'

'No?'

'Change partners, of course! I think Rebecca and Marc get on quite well together. Look, they're just going out to one of the balconies.'

'In that case. . .'

'Say no more, Susy. Why don't we simply leave while they're otherwise engaged? A message can be left at the desk, and they can get a taxi for themselves.'

'Why not? Let's go before we change our minds!'

They went to a small exclusive nightclub that Ross knew, the sort of place that opened at ten in the evening and closed at five the following morning. The ambience was even more seductive; low lights sent splashes of gold about the room, and there was smoochy music for couples who seemed only to want to stand still in each other's arms. Everything was geared for bewitching allurement.

'Have we come to the right place?' Susy murmured, as they made their way to one of the few remaining tables, its surface holding lamplit flowers, leaving just enough room for two glasses.

'Of course,' Ross said, taking her arm, noticing several appreciative males eyeing Susy. They sat down, Ross ordering wine, then leaning across the table towards her. 'Did you think I'd brought you to a place that might be raided by the police at any minute?'

Her laughter transformed her face, and her chandelier earrings trembled. 'Ross! Now that really would be exciting!' She glanced around at the tasteful décor: the gilt furniture; the pop group in evening dress; the women's expensive-looking dresses. 'Has it ever happened here?'

He shrugged. 'I've been a member for several years and haven't seen it yet. Oh, my God!' he exclaimed suddenly. 'My ex-wife's over there with one of her boyfriends — the dark-haired girl in the cream evening gown. I don't want her to join us tonight, Susy; I wanted this to be. . .well, just us. She hasn't seen us yet; do you mind if we leave?'

'No, of course not,' Susy murmured, taking a quick peep at the girl she'd heard so much about.

Ross was already shepherding her out to the foyer.

'What about coming back to my place for a drink? it's quite near here.'

'Well — er. . .I'm. . .' she stammered, as they waited outside for a taxi.

Ross broke in with a laugh, 'I'm only asking you back for a drink, Susy. No ulterior motives, I assure you.'

He wouldn't have been quite so certain had he known how with one touch he could collapse all her good intentions. Despite everything, she still could not shake off the fatal attraction for him that refused to let her go. 'It's not that, Ross,' she said, surprised to hear that her voice sounded quite normal. 'Anyhow, I'm no longer Mummy and Daddy's little girl, if you remember?' she teased.

He clasped her hand as they got into the taxi, and in minutes, it seemed, they had drawn up outside a red-brick house at the end of a long gravel drive. It was two-storey, with a white front door, and large pine trees all around protecting it from the sea which could be heard rushing up on to the shingle.

Inside, the house seemed to ooze comfort and well-being. He showed her into a small sitting-room. 'This is my "den",' he smiled. 'Just comfortable chairs, good books, and a drinks cabinet!'

She smiled, looking admiringly at the several oil paintings of full-rigged sailing ships on the walls, the deep leather armchairs and bowls of flowers obviously arranged by the caring housekeeper he often mentioned.

'I think it's great.'

'Be truthful, and tell me it's obvious a bachelor lives here!'

'I was admiring those lovely old cargo ships, actually.'

'Glad you like them. Now, glass of wine?'

They sat talking about the house mostly until he

said, 'I was sorry about our leaving the nightclub, Susy,
but I know Miriam, and she would have insisted we all
join up together. As you'd had rather a long day, I
thought it might be rather too much. After all, she
doesn't have to get up and go to work tomorrow.'

She smiled. 'You're right. Today has been rather. . .
different.'

'Did you enjoy the cocktail party?'

'Yes, thanks. Staff let me get away early. She's such
a nice person.'

'Yes, she has rather a struggle trying to bring up two
wayward sons, I believe. On her own too.'

'How rotten, I didn't know.'

'A smile often conceals a load of unhappiness,' Ross
muttered thoughtfully, then put the subject aside. 'By
the way, how are you feeling about your interview for
the job on Friday? All your papers are with us, of
course. I think you stand a good chance.'

'Thanks, Ross. I certainly don't want any preferential treatment,' she said firmly, her eyes looking frankly
into his.

'Forget that, Susy. If you want this job enough and
feel confident you can do it, that's all I'm concerned
with.'

He took her empty glass, put it on a side-table and
sat next to her on the triple settee, his eyes holding
hers. 'You look quite lovely tonight, do you know
that?'

She smiled back at him. 'A compliment like that is
rare for me these days! Thank you, Ross.'

He took her hand, his eyes going to the circle of pale
skin on the third finger of her left hand. 'I mean it.' He
looked back at her. 'I think you're one of those people
who is capable of coming through a big let-down and
its attendant stress, with honours which show — to your
advantage — in your face.'

She would never know if it was the alcohol she'd had

that evening, but she realised that tears had welled into her eyes and her lips quivered hopelessly as she tried vainly to say, 'It's generous of you to give me such a morale-booster, Ross.' She tried to stem the flow with her fingers. 'But. . .but. . .' She floundered, still unable to put him right about Patrick. 'Sorry, I'm wilting!'

He dabbed her eyes with a pristine white handkerchief from his pocket, showing the same tenderness he used on the children. 'You know, Susy, I think you're a little overwrought because this has been a long session for you.' He pressed his lips to her forehead suddenly, seeing her lovely eyes as bright as diamonds, while his lips travelled down to hers, the contact gentle and without passion.

'Ross,' she murmured, 'you're such a good friend.'

'Marc and I do our best,' he said, moving from her slightly and wagging an admonishing finger. 'He and I both agree how much better you seem lately, but one thing I believe, and that is you should put all past misery aside and one day fall in love again. That's my prescription for you, for what it's worth!' He stood up suddenly with a smile. 'I'm also going to ring for a taxi; you must be tired, and the falling in love thing can wait!'

They returned to her home in the car. On the doorstep he kissed her gently goodnight. 'Thank you for making it such a lovely evening, Susy. Maybe we'll get around to another some time.'

She stood listening to the sound of the vehicle as it went off down the drive, her mind still on Ross, yet her subconscious thoughts were on Patrick, as they were most of the time. Only that morning Susy had received a letter from his mother, and, as well as news of their family, had mentioned that she had been to see Father O'Hara about Patrick's memorial service. It had not been possible before until some of his relatives were able to arrange to come over from South Africa, and now it seemed plans were under way.

She glanced up at the velvety sky, not wanting to go indoors. The sweet-smelling countryside was sleeping, silence blanketed the whole world briefly, it seemed. The stars above were bright, yet so far away — unattainable, rather as were her own mixed thoughts about her deep attraction towards Ross Beaumaris.

She wandered slowly beneath the trees that skirted the edge of the lawn, her mind in a turmoil over the man to whom she had been drawn so readily, and yet wasn't she diving in at the deep end by applying to work for him? Surely it had to be a crazy situation, but she knew something was goading her on to try for the job. After so many months of hesitation and fear, she was convinced in her heart that she was at last able to see clearly that this was the path she must take, whatever the outcome.

She didn't hear or see the car until it slid to a stop outside the gate. It was Ross; she would know his tall, distinguished figure anywhere. He walked up the path, a smile on his face when he saw her, a silvery moon riding high in the sky above him.

'Ross!' She moved towards him. 'Is something wrong?'

He gave a soft laugh. 'No, only my memory! Your father asked me earlier tonight if I would pass you your garage key so that you could get away early in the morning, thinking they might oversleep after a late night. I only thought of it as I reached the farm at the end of the lane.'

'Thank you. . .it's good of you. . .' she stammered, very much aware of his nearness, his eyes gazing at her as if mesmerised.

'My God, but you look beautiful. . .' he murmured, lifting a hand and brushing her cheek. 'I don't know which outshines the other, your skin or the moonlight.'

She felt a great rush of pleasure and emotion at seeing him, having subconsciously felt, when at his house earlier, that his tenderness and concern for her had put some of his more flirtatious intentions from his mind. Again she had experienced a twinge of conscience, knowing that at the close of their evening together it might have been rather different had she not hesitated about Patrick. In fact that was what she really wanted—the selfish, wild clamouring of her blood whenever Ross was near—and already at this moment she knew it was a losing battle again. They stood looking at each other, as she murmured huskily, 'Moonlight can be deceptive, Ross. . .'

'Never. . .' His firm lips brushed hers, yet with the lightness of a moth's wing, sending a reaction like surf pounding on a beach racing through her. All she wanted was his arms about her, even tighter than they already were. She closed her eyes, revelling in the sensuous caress of his mouth as he sent small, dangerously potent kisses over every contour and plane of her face, then slowly, but deliberately, returning to the warm, moist beauty of her lips that waited for him. Every muscle in his body blended with the soft, supple pliancy of her own, creating a desire so intense within her, such a dizzying welter of heightened emotions, that subconsciously she knew she should draw back lest this man, this comparative stranger, become a complete obsession with her.

She turned her head to one side, trying to move from his urgent embrace, wanting to regain a semblance of normality before making an utter fool of herself. 'Ross. . . I must go now. . .' Thank heaven he had no idea how physically drawn she was to him. It had to be that. She hardly knew him outside the hospital, apart from which, if he was to become her superior, she needed all the self-possession and pride she could muster.

His arms dropped from her, a taut smile on his face. 'Sorry, Susy. All my good intentions suddenly escaped me when I saw you here in the garden. That little black dress of yours was a show-stopper tonight, but out here in the moonlight it turns you into a goddess.'

She laughed softly, trying to break the tension. 'Don't get too physical, Ross! Most girls have a little black dress for certain occasions, but they can't always conjure up the moonlight as well!'

He grinned back. 'You mean it's like having too many favourite chocolates all in one box!'

'Something like that.' She took the garage key that he held out to her. 'Goodnight now. Thanks so much for a lovely evening, Ross.'

'Night, Susy, sleep well.' He turned to wave at the gate. 'But I still love that dress!'

Indoors she took a warm shower and rested rather than slept — there was hardly any time for that — and besides, she would have quite definitely overslept. At eleven that morning she went to see Miss Aldridge about her interview that had been arranged for the following day.

Miss Aldridge allowed a small frown to disturb the smoothness of her brow. 'Oh, dear, of course, and that only leaves us with the two young nurses on Ortho, and it's Mason's day off tomorrow.' She stood up from her desk suddenly. 'However, that's not for you to worry about, Susy. I'll do a bit of reshuffling with Julia on Medical; she can divide her shifts between the two main wards. I should start to call Ortho Orchid now, shouldn't I?' she said, with a smiling reference to the newly christened ward.

Julia and Susy met in the common-room that morning for coffee and talked of Miss Aldridge's intentions.

'Oh, I don't mind for a change, Frenais,' Julia said brightly. 'But what I'm dying to know is what happened

when John and I saw that American guy spiriting you
away from the cocktail party with Ross and Rebecca.'

'Oh, that! It was great; we all went out to dinner
together.'

'And. . .' Julia's eyes twinkled with devilment.

'No *and*, Julia; then we split up and went our
separate ways afterwards.'

'With the American, you mean?' Julia burst into a
gale of laughter. 'Susy, don't look so worried; you're
old enough to go out with whoever you like! Anyway,
I just hope you had a wonderful time, that's all!'

Susy had hedged over the real truth of the matter
last evening. She wanted to hug it to herself, and that
alone made it quite an unusual occurrence between
herself and Julia. But it was that final kiss in the
moonlight with Ross that made her hold back. For
some reason she wanted to share it with no one.

Certainly Julia didn't appear to be worried, and was
already leaping on to another topic altogether. 'Have I
mentioned the name Robert Sloan?'

'No.'

'Well, he's one of the new young housemen over in
General. He's only been here a week and practically
drowned himself getting cut off by the tide quite near
where you live actually. He took a small rowing boat
out to one of the coves along there, then realised the
tide was more treacherous than he thought. His boat
capsized, he tried to swim for it, but apparently the
currents kept hurling him back against the rocks. He
was in a pretty bad state, and if it hadn't been for old
Ross out for an afternoon sail he might have been a
gonner. He spent last night recovering on one of our
side-wards.' She grinned. 'Trouble is, he fancies himself as a right little Romeo. God, talk about conceited!'

'What does he look like?'

'Blond, fairly tall, bit of a snappy dresser. I dare say

you'll run across him sooner or later. Bit of a twit really, though.' She glanced up at the wall clock. 'I must fly; I think Miss Aldridge is due for one of her Gestapo inspections this afternoon!'

CHAPTER NINE

'ANYONE at home this afternoon?'

Ross bowled in to the ward office, arriving later than usual, and grinned at Susy, who he thought looked as fresh as a daisy. There was a speck of blood on his jaw, as if he'd shaved in a hurry and hadn't had time to notice. 'Hi, Susy! Don't tell me! I knew it was going to be a bad day when my electric shaver packed up.'

'Rough luck!' She laughed. 'Worse things happen at sea!'

'I suppose so! You all set for the fray tomorrow, Susy, no second thoughts?'

'None at all,' she declared firmly.

'Splendid.' He turned to pick up one of the files on the desk, catching sight of his face in the wall mirror. 'Good lord! I didn't realise I'd been walking about like this since I arrived. Be a love and find me some spirit, will you?'

She was already at the cupboard for cotton wool. 'Stand still, please.' She grinned as he moved closer to her, obediently raising his chin while she dabbed the speck away, his nearness switching on its old seduction. She said the first thing that came into her head. 'That scar. . .how did you manage to get it?'

'A present from Miriam, when she took to hurling brandy glasses around occasionally! More importantly, I like your gentle touch, Nurse; I shall have to remember that at the interview tomorrow!' he teased. 'Even so, that stunning little black dress you wore last night took some beating!'

'Dr Beaumaris,' she grinned, 'that was yesterday;

this is today, which incidentally, if you remember, you forecast was going to be a bad one!'

He gave an exaggerated sigh, clipping a pen into the top pocket of his white coat. 'Well, I could be wrong — for once!' he chuckled, as they set off with the trolley of files for Orchid Ward. 'Still, maybe the rest of the day has possibilities after all; someone has actually displayed the name of our newly christened ward. I hope they remember the other one.'

'The party at the Atlantic will have been in vain if they don't!'

'I want to look at the little girl, Merry, with the fractured skull, or at least a suspected fissure. From the night report she appears to have had a decent night.'

Before she had time to answer they were entering the ward, brightly coloured and hung with mobiles, the children calling their, 'Good morning, Dr Ross!' in a choir of excitable treble voices.

After Ross had acknowledged the ecstatic welcome, they reached Merry's bed. Susy said, 'She seems fairly subdued at the moment; her mother was in this morning but had to leave early.'

Ross smiled at the flaxen-haired child. 'Hi, Merry, that's a nice book you have there. Who bought it for you? I really like those stand-up pictures.'

'My mummy bought it for me, and if I'm good she's going to buy me another one.'

Ross was running his hands skilfully over the child's head. 'Do you know, I have an idea that you've decided to be very, very good? Are you looking forward to going home soon?'

Her blue eyes shone as, clutching her book, she rocked her head up and down. 'Yes.'

'Well, that's positive, anyway. We'll be talking to Mummy and Daddy when they come in this afternoon.'

As they left the bedside, Ross murmured to Susy, 'I

think she's OK to go tomorrow, I didn't want to raise her hopes too high; another night in hospital is a long time to a child.'

They moved away from the bed. 'Just to recap on Merry's notes, we know there's no skull fracture, she's alert, had no vomiting, headache or amnesia. From what we know, the home conditions are suitable, the mother's intelligent and aware of the symptoms of deterioration if it occurs. I'll check that there's a phone in the house or near by, and that their GP is informed once Merry's discharged. That could be tomorrow. I'll see her in the morning before she goes.' He replaced his pen in his white coat pocket, then added as an afterthought, 'If it does happen that both parents come back this afternoon, I'll have a word with them.'

They moved across to Kevin's bed. Ross stopped again, taking up his file, murmuring, 'Now, let's see; the lad's been having passive stretching and active exercise as well as regular sessions of head traction.' Ross put the file aside, smiling at Kevin. He was sitting out in a chair, bathed and dressed, with a cheeky smile on his face. Ross playfully nuzzled his fist into the boy's chin. 'Hi! You've been a jolly good chap, you know. How do you fancy going home quite soon now?'

'Oh, yes, please, then my mum's going to take me to see Robin, where he lives.'

'That sounds terrific.' Ross removed the padded collar from the child's neck, assessing progress. 'The physiotherapist will be coming to see you each day, Kevin, from now on, and she's going to get you to look in a mirror each morning to make certain you're holding your head correctly.' In an aside to Rosa who had just joined them, he explained, 'For a torticollis deformity, at this stage, re-education in front of a mirror is given until the child has postural sense to keep the head straight by reflex, and supervision will be continued after discharge. In this case another week to ten days at most.'

Kevin was looking very perky after Susy had fastened on his collar again. 'Can I go and play now, Nurse Susy?'

'Yes, off you go!'

After Ross had left, Susy sat working on the Kardex now that the children were about to have their eleven o'clock drinks. She tried hard to concentrate, but it was difficult when she thought of the following day and how much the job of staff nurse meant to her. It wasn't only her personal belief in herself, but she wanted to prove both to her father and to Ross that she was quite recovered and well able to take on the responsibility that might be offered her. And yet she still remembered Ross's provocative words in the first place, although he had tempered his attitude somewhat since then, but she would give anything to know what was behind his reasoning.

She sighed, pushing the forms aside. It was time she made sure that all was well with the five young patients on Fraser. Two junior nurses and the schoolteacher were there, and Susy was told that the SNO had also called in on the same mission. So the staff shortage was not at this moment causing any great inconvenience. Suddenly hearing a plane streaking up into the sky reminded her that her parents were leaving for their holiday soon now. The house was beginning to look as if it were being packed for removal despite her helping her mother make copious lists. Still deep in thought, she walked out to the corridor and vaguely heard someone say, 'I don't believe it!' A young, white-coated man was staring at her open-mouthed. 'I say! I'm terribly sorry. . .' His eyes roamed over her apron 'Miss — um —— Can I help?'

Thank heaven Julie had already warned her. This must be Robert Sloan. She grinned at him, his face

quite dumbstruck when she showed no amazement,
saying, 'Hi! How are you liking it here?'

He laughed, looking slightly embarrassed. 'Well, it's
only been for a very short time so far. You may have
heard I practically got myself drowned; would have but
for Dr Beaumaris.' His grey eyes went over her. 'Still,
lucky for me I strayed into the wrong ward by mistake.'
He looked at her identity brooch. 'Ah, Susy Frenais! I
do hope we meet again!'

Susy smiled. 'Forgive me, I'm in rather a hurry. See
you around!' She didn't need any more complications.

She soon forgot the incident, and later arranged with
Miss Aldridge that she should leave an hour earlier
that afternoon in order to have a little more time to
herself before the interview next day. As she drove
home, Ross was still on her mind, his charm, the
pleasurable company and ready wit, apart from his
other attractions. But when he was on the selection
committee, as he would be next day, she knew she
could expect no special considerations — not that she
wanted them — but there were times when she had
witnessed him in certain situations when he could be
very formidable indeed.

Once back at home, she was in her bedroom when
the phone rang. It was Marc. 'Hi, Susy; sorry I've been
otherwise engaged lately, but I hadn't forgotten about
tomorrow, and I wondered if you'd like to go out
somewhere for a quiet dinner. Don't worry, I'll see
we're back in plenty of time!'

'Well, that's a great idea, Marc, thank you. I can
think of nothing I'd like better.'

'Terrific; I'll pick you up at seven.'

An hour later Ross rang. 'Susy, can you make dinner
with me tonight, just to take your mind off things?'

'Well. . .it's kind of you, Ross, but I've already made
an arrangement, I'm afraid.'

His voice was curt. 'I see; I had a feeling this might happen. I imagine it's Marc.'

'Yes, but——'

He cut in abruptly, 'OK, that's fine; it was just an idea. Have a good evening. Bye now.'

Slowly she replaced the receiver. He sounded so cold, as if she'd purposely contrived to disappoint him. Then she dashed the foolish thought away; why should she feel this way when he was just a friend and colleague, nothing more? He surely couldn't be jealous, he wasn't the type, and besides, there was nothing between them that could warrant it. And, if as he no doubt thought, there was a kind of understanding with herself and Marc. . .well, it was damned well nothing to do with him!

She dined again with Marc at his hotel in St Helier, the quiet understated luxury was just the sort of thing that was immediately calming and relaxing. Marc was saying, as they exchanged news. 'By the way, I'll soon be returning to the States — unfortunately my stay here has to be shorter than I thought.'

'Marc, I'm really sorry. Does Rebecca know?'

He frowned. 'Why? What has she got to do with it?'

'Well, I thought that you and she were. . .well, getting along together,' she finished lamely.

He gave one of his quietly amused grins. 'No, not me, honey. As I once told you, I've tried to start again once or twice, but it just doesn't work. No, me? I'm just a one-woman guy, I guess. How is the boy Robin, by the way?'

'He's doing well really, Marc, but he doesn't take kindly to too much moving around.'

'Well, that's understandable, poor little kid.'

A waiter appeared at that particular moment and Marc ordered coffee and liquers as they moved into the residents' lounge.

When they were comfortably settled, from then on

Marc's mind seemed fixed on other, more personal things. He said with a gleam in his eye, 'Don't forget now, Susy, don't turn into an oldie like me and give up all thought of ever finding love again. I know one or two people who would be only too delighted to have you just look their way.'

She smiled, staring down at her ringless hand.

'I don't think so, Marc. As *you* know, it has to be the right kind of love, and that doesn't appear too often.'

When they left the hotel and Marc saw her home in a cab, on her doorstep he brushed his lips across her forehead. 'You just sock it to 'em tomorrow, babe. I know you'll do it!'

'Thanks, Marc, you'll bring me luck!'

'I'm darned sure I will. Bye now!'

Next morning Susy dressed with care in a classic silk *café-au-lait* shirtdress that she had worn once on a happier occasion, and as she went downstairs for her mother's approval she hoped it might bring her luck.

Looking at Susy, with her hair swept up in a shining twist at the back of her head, brown eyes luminous with determination, Dorothy Frenais's heart swelled with pride at the sight of her daughter. At the front door she waved her off in the car, unyielding in her decision that on no account would she have told Susy about the phone call from the home half an hour ago, to say that a childless couple had arranged to take young Robin into their home for the first of several weekends with a view to adoption.

The interview was over. Susy had been called back to face the committee, and the coveted job had been offered to her, starting the following day in view of the extenuating circumstances. Having accepted in a daze of happiness and satisfaction, Susy left the boardroom walking on air, still thinking of some of the questions that had been put to her. Smooth comments suddenly switched for her to give an analysis of the point at hand; opinions they elicited on the current state of her profession and if it was keeping up with the times; if there was any area in particular where she would want changes. The fact that her father and Ross Beaumaris were putting some of these very questions had quickly banished in Susy's head any thoughts of nepotism as far as her father was concerned; it only served to put her even more on her mettle.

Outside the boardroom, Ross appeared. 'Susy, well done! Congratulations!' he called, taking her hand and shaking it again, having already done so with the rest of the panel in a more formal fashion. All coolness from last evening was completely gone. 'Come along to the senior common-room and have another cup of tea; it'll taste much better than the one you had earlier! Your father and the rest of them are still mulling on the appointment of the other candidates. I think those two new RGN's are going to be most suitable.'

'Ross, this is nice of you, but I could go straight home, you know.'

'No, not a bit of it. You need to relax before you leave. The thing that I'm so delighted with is that it must put the seal on the complete renewal of your confidence! You did yourself proud this morning.'

They talked about her new status and the attendant changes, such as money, uniform, hours, holidays, until at last she stood up to leave. 'I can't take up any more of your time, Ross; I must get back now. I promised to take young Robin out this afternoon.'

'This afternoon?' he repeated sharply.

'Yes,' she said, wondering why he should sound so amazed. 'Well, it is OK, isn't it? I mean, you hadn't planned to go and see him; it's not your day for the children?'

A shadow seemed to pass across his face. 'Look, Susy, sit down again. Seeing that you've mentioned Robin, there's something I want to tell you.'

'There's nothing wrong with him?' she asked anxiously.

'No, of course not. He's fine now, but it's about adoption.'

'Oh, no! I wish I'd gone to see him earlier. I thought he was over that. He seemed to throw it off a few days after he left the hospital. Matron said she could see the improvement, and I dare say Sandra has. . .'

Ross placed a gently restraining hand on her arm. 'Susy, just listen to me for a minute. It has nothing to do with that. There's an eminently suitable couple who are interested in adopting the boy. Apparently their background's impeccable, everything's been checked out. Now it just remains for them all to get to know each other. You know, of course, that this takes a very long time, maybe two years or so before everyone's satisfied, but the fact remains, integration into the new home and family environment has to start some time, and I wanted to tell you early in the proceedings so that *you* can become used to the idea, as well as Robin. I know how much he means to you and I don't want either you or him getting hurt.'

She was shocked at the news, but tried to keep herself in check. 'Thanks, Ross,' she said quietly. 'I'm glad it was you who told me. Perhaps I have tended to think I've some sort of prior claim on him. I'll speak to Mum about it tonight, although knowing her she probably wouldn't mention it until today was over. . .' he saw the telltale brilliance in her eyes '. . .but. . . I'll. . . I'll. . . .'

Ross said quickly, 'You'll simply carry on as you have so far, but let him go from your heart and mind gradually, Susy. I'm not unfeeling, but, being a child,

he won't even realise it once he begins to notice the
two people who want to be his parents.'

She bit her lip, not speaking.

'So, what's happening tonight, then? Great celebrations, I hope?' he said with forced gaiety. 'Remember your promise to step up the smiles! You're on my
staff now, Susy Frenais, and smiling is one of my first
house rules!'

She managed an apology of a smile, grateful for his
understanding. 'As a matter of fact, Mum and Dad had
planned to take me out tonight, seeing that they're
leaving for the cruise tomorrow morning. It's great;
they're like a couple of schoolchildren.'

'Yes, Ian told me, actually; they deserve a wonderful
time. I just hope I can keep the young housemen in
check as well as your father does. One Robert Sloan in
particular.'

Susy looked at him quizzically. 'The one who nearly
got himself drowned but for you! Is he very trouble-
some, then?'

'Young blood, I suppose; he needs reining in. His
ego's rather too much for him at present!'

On the drive home Susy called in at St Helier's
market for some shopping, still smiling at Ross's words
about Robert Sloan. That young man had a lot to learn
if he thought he could put anything over on Ross,
especially while her father was away!

As she parked the car in the garage at home, her
mother came hurrying out and threw her arms round
her. 'Congratulations, darling! I could hardly sit still all
morning until I knew. Your father rang, and since he
came home just now he's been giving me a minute-by-
minute account of the whole proceedings!' She looked
at her daughter with great compassion. 'He also told
me that Ross was going to mention Robin to you. It's
best for him, darling, isn't it?'

Indoors her father was ready with the celebratory

drinks. They raised their glasses to her. 'To new beginnings, Susy,' Ian said proudly.

'Hear, hear!' Dorothy echoed. 'You've made a perfect recovery, Susy; I just wish they could see you now in Belfast. Incidentally, there's a letter upstairs for you from Patrick's parents.'

'Thanks, Mum, I'll see it later, and thanks to you both for all you've done for me. Now, here's to a wonderful holiday. May it be the best ever.'

The following day at the hospital Susy spent most of the morning with Miss Aldridge. She had slept little after the excitement of the day before but now, as she tapped on the SNO's door, deep down in her subconscious she was trying to fight off, no longer fear of doing her job, but a severe case of normal butterflies.

Miss Aldridge opened the door to her with a smile. 'Come along in, my dear; do sit down.'

A tray of coffee and biscuits was set ready on an occasional table between them, and gradually Susy began to overcome her initial nervousness.

'Bureaucracy being what it is, Susy,' Miss Aldridge said pleasantly, pouring the coffee and handing her a cup, 'your transition from voluntary helper to being established on our staff as a fully-fledged staff nurse is, as you can imagine, going to involve much form-filling and various other requirements; but that will all be completed in the fullness of time. However, I thought we could spend a short while on such things as regulations, hours, uniform, salary and suchlike. Later, I'll take you for a tour over the hospital, which you've not had recently, and introduce you to some of the staff who will be useful to you in future. Firstly, though, I have some uniform dresses here from which you can select your own size. Sometimes it's necessary, or rather preferable, to wear white cotton trousers and jackets, more in Theatre than anywhere, I suppose. As you know, uniform caps are no longer considered to be essential except on certain occasions. As far as our children are concerned, especially the very young ones, informality is the watchword. A flowered cover-up or apron is often a good enough substitute when necessary.

The morning sped by quickly, and by the time the two parted company, with Miss Aldridge's good wishes for the future ringing in her ears, Susy at long last felt an integral part of the hospital and the work she had come to love.

With so much going on, it was several days before Susy remembered that she had a birthday coming up in four days' time, her twenty-sixth. With the novelty of having the house to herself, her parents away, and the new job totally absorbing her time, time seemed of little consequence. Ross had been his usual helpful self, although two evenings ago when Marc had invited her out to a celebration dinner, including Ross, he had claimed to have another commitment. It seemed as if the easy friendship that had developed between them before Susy had taken on the new job had somehow frozen into a more aloof relationship. He was complimentary enough at first, as were her friends, but Susy couldn't shake off the feeling that now she actually worked directly for him and had proved she was completely recovered he was putting distance between them.

She told herself that it wasn't worrying her one little bit, but then at unguarded moments she would remember the kisses, the odd slanging match they'd had, the apologies, the tenderness, all of which seemed to hammer away at her brain more than ever just lately. That morning she met Julia for coffee, and was busily telling her friend about the forgotten birthday. 'So, I thought I'd throw a party at home and invite everyone at the hospital who'd like to come! How does that sound?'

'Terrific, Susy; I'll get some of the other girls to come and give a hand with the grub. We can get together and work out what we want. Hey, tell you something else! John's got these three blokes he plays badminton with; they're just setting up their own pop group and they're terrific apparently. Would you like me to ask John if he'll see whether they're free?'

'Great! But just a minute, if it's going to be the Saturday following my birthday, wouldn't they be fixed up for the weekend?'

Julia giggled. 'I'll tell John to make sure they're not! They're relying upon him to turn them into Jersey badminton champs, as well as hopes for world success musically!'

'I'll leave that to you, then. How about tomorrow evening for coming to my place and we'll work out some lists?'

'Suits me fine.'

On the ward that afternoon, Susy told Rosa what was in hand when she arrived for her shift.

'We have a young boy of six coming in with an elbow fracture. He's been X-rayed and will be going to Theatre at any time for plastering. I'm apparently wanted to help out until we get our new theatre sister, so there's plenty to do.'

Susy had been mildly surprised to be asked by Ross that morning to help out with this particular case; her basic theatre training had been some time ago, but apart from that she felt apprehensive that he had demanded her presence as a kind of retribution for not having dinner with him on the night before her job interview. Now, she wondered how long he intended . . .the phone broke into her thoughts, and she was asked to report to Dr Beaumaris in Theatre Two.

On arrival outside the rest-room for relatives, the six-year-old's mother sat looking terrified. 'Excuse me, Nurse, are you going into the theatre with my little boy? Well, he's already in there, but I mean will you be staying?'

'Hello, Mrs Hall, isn't it?' Susy smiled.

The woman nodded miserably. 'Yes.'

'I'll be with Grant the whole time, Mrs Hall. As a matter of fact, he'll be on my ward. I'm Staff Nurse Frenais. Try not to worry; I'll see you again as soon as we've finished.'

Inside the main theatre the child was already anaesthetised, all checks made. Ross looked up at Susy's entrance. 'I thought this would be good experience for you, Staff,' he said formally, dark eyes holding hers above his mask. 'The patient's ready now to go into the plaster-room.'

Ross stood back and watched the careful transference of the child. Only when Ross had satisfied himself that the plaster operator knew the five points necessary before a plaster was applied did he have the boy transferred to the Hawley table. Not until the child was placed in the desired position and certain padding fixed into place did he give instructions for the first bandage to be handed to the operator.

Ross's eyes met hers. 'Have you come across a supracondylar fracture like this one before, Staff?'

'Not in practical terms, no, I haven't.' She cursed her luck that she hadn't thought to check such an injury in one of the textbooks in the office.

'Well, perhaps you'd like to tell me what you do know about it?' The dark blue orbs were almost navy that afternoon, and she knew she was right—he was in one of his arrogant moods as he waited for her response.

She took a deep breath. 'Textually, this particular injury is a fracture of the humerus. Um. . .with regard to the fracture itself, the X-ray will have shown the position of the bone ends. The lower fragment is usually displaced backwards, and the jagged edge of the upper fragment causes damage to the brachial artery, and sometimes to the median nerve.'

'And the thing to watch when plastering?'

'Well. . .' She gulped, racking her brains for a last vestige of recollection about something she hadn't dealt with for ages. 'After immobilising the limb in plaster of Paris, a window must be cut at the wrist in order to feel the radial pulse, and should be recorded every fifteen minutes.'

'Right, Staff, I think that will do for now,' Ross said dismissively, watching the operator trim off the plaster edges with a sharp knife, finishing by turning the padding back ready to be secured with a plaster band or strapping when dry. The child was then returned to the recovery-room, where Ross reassured the mother, and said that she could stay with her son now that he was showing signs of returning to consciousness. Ross came back into the ante-theatre where Susy was discarding her protective clothing. 'Staff, leave Nurse with the young lad and his mother once he's round completely, and just ring Staff Mason to say your patient is on his way up.' He was tugging off his gown. 'I want a word before you go, please,' he said shortly.

When she had carried out his instructions she followed Ross into the private office off the theatre, to find he was leaning nonchalantly against a table, in his shirt-sleeves and beige twill trousers that clung expensively to his slim hips. He was studying a folder, but put it aside when she appeared, folding his arms across his chest. It gave him a formidable air, and she wondered if, now that her father was away for two weeks, he intended demonstrating a little more of the inner depths she suspected. Yet he seemed less officious suddenly, leaving only a weariness across his good-looking features, and she couldn't help feeling a pang of smypathy for him. She knew he had already performed four ops earlier that day, two of them major for private patients in the main building. And being responsible also for setting up a new wing worth many thousands of pounds was no small anxiety. Now, he ran a hand across some tell-tale stubble on his chin, saying, 'I just wanted to make sure you're not going to find the pace of the new job too frantic?'

'No, not at all.'

'Thank heaven for that. I know there's a lot to absorb with the added responsibility you now have, and it's early days yet, but I want you to promise me that if you find things heavy going in these first few weeks you'll let me know and I'll see what I can do to ease matters.'

'It's very good of you, Ross, thank you. But really I'm more than optimistic about the future now.'

'Good girl. But don't overdo it.'

She smiled. 'By the way, Ross——' she kept her fingers crossed behind her back '—I'm giving a party next Saturday at home, and am inviting any of the hospital staff who care to come, yourself included. Will you think about it?'

'Thanks, I certainly will. A celebration for your achievement is it?' he grinned.

'Well, of a different sort, really. I'm another year older. I'll be twenty-six on Tuesday!'

'My God, what an advanced age! Knowing that, wild horses wouldn't keep me away!'

Susy laughed, glancing up at the clock. 'That's great, Ross. I'm going to see Robin for a little while now, once I've been home.'

A shadow passed across his face. 'Have you cleared it with Matron?'

'Yes. She said I could still take him out. Her exact words were that the more varied the people who do so, the easier it will be for him to. . .well. . .sort of become acclimatised to any new surroundings.'

As she left the building, Ross stood looking out of

the window, thinking of Susy and Robin. It disturbed
him greatly that both of them would be hurt; it was
bound to happen. And with Susy still burdened with
some part of her life of which he knew very little, he
could see trouble ahead.

The afternoon for Susy was a great joy. She and Robin
spent two hours on the beach, having a picnic tea and
then sitting together trying to identify the sea-birds
who wanted to share it.

Robin was definitely in one of his enquiring moods
that day, and after a long talk about Sandra and the
new parents who came to collect her each weekend he
said suddenly, 'I'd like you to be my mummy, Susy.
Would *you* like that?'

'Well, I've never been a real mummy, Robin. I
mean, I haven't been married and had any children
yet.'

'You could get married, though, and then have me.
Why haven't you been married?'

'I've been engaged to be married, but we decided
. . .we decided not to, after all.'

'I wish you hadn't, Susy, 'cos I love you.'

She swallowed hard. 'The people who want to adopt
you love you, too, darling.'

'Yes, but I don't love them,' he said logically. He
turned his head suddenly. 'Oh, look at that big seagull,
Susy, he's pecking at the little one for taking that cake.
He's greedy, isn't he?'

When Susy got home that evening she rang Matron
and gave her the gist of the conversation. 'I think at
the moment, my dear, we'll take all of that with a pinch
of salt. Once Robin has become used to other people
being fond of him, there'll be changes, I'm quite sure.'

And, getting ready for bed that night, Susy wished
her mother had been at home just to talk things over.

CHAPTER TEN

LATE Friday afternoon, the day before the birthday
party, the telephone rang on Fraser ward, and Susy
made a grimace as news of a late admission came
through. Casualty Sister sounded rushed. 'We're sending you a young patient, Staff, suspected acute osteo-
myelitis, pain in the left femur. High temp. Dr
Beaumaris has been told; he'll be coming to see the
child as soon as possible. Name: Wendy Moore, aged
eight. Mother will be visiting after work. That's it for
now. Thanks very much.' And the phone cut off
abruptly.

Thankful that Rosa was still on duty with her, Susy,
together with the hardworking young girl, finished
preparing the child's bed just as the porter arrived with
his charge and handed Susy the details. 'There we are,
Staff; she's not going to let the night nurse have much
sleep tonight, I don't think!' he quipped, looking quite
amused at such a corny old joke.

Susy frowned at the little girl's flushed face and
restless appearance as she lay on the trolley. 'OK,
John, bring her over here, will you?'

After settling Wendy into bed, Susy took her tem-
perature which was up to forty degrees Celsius or a
hundred and four Fahrenheit, the pulse was rapid and
her tongue was furred. Every now and then she burst
into incoherent mumbling. Susy smoothed back the
child's damp brown curls from her face. 'Why on earth
couldn't the mother have come in and stayed?' she
muttered almost to herself. 'The child's delirious.
Rosa, would you apply some cold compresses to her

head, please, while I go and see if I can contact Dr
Beaumaris?'

As she was about to go into the office, Ross suddenly
burst through the outer doors. 'Wendy Moore, Susy —
you have her settled in, I believe?'

'Yes, she's very miserable.'

They went to the bedside, Susy drawing back the
curtains to reveal the child's feverish condition. Ross
scanned her notes. 'Complaining of pain at the top of
her left leg. Wouldn't allow anyone near it without
screaming. Relatives?' he said to Susy, while gently
running his hands over the child's limbs.

'The mother apparently came in with her in the
ambulance, but had to go to work. Single parent. She'll
be in again later tonight.'

'Oh, dear. . .' Ross shook his head despairing
'. . .and this poor child's going to be here with us for
quite a while yet by the look of things.'

Susy nodded sympathetically. 'With my father away,
have you a locum?'

'Yes, Dr le Clerc from the children's hospital on the
other side of town. Good man; he'll be helping out
until Ian's back, and there are two fairly new peds
housemen who'll be useful.'

'Fine.' Susy covered the crying child, making sure
the bed cradle supported the bedclothes away from the
afflicted leg.

Ross felt the child's pulse. 'I shall want blood taken
for culture now to identify the organism and determine
how sensitive it is to antibiotics. The bottle must be
sent to the lab at once. These children are often
anaemic so we'll need to estimate the haemoglobin
level. However, we'll repeat all tests later, although no
changes will be visible for the first ten to twelve days.
We'll leave the X-rays until tomorrow when she's
settled down a little. Meantime I'll give her something
mild to make her sleep, until we can get her started on

the antibiotics in large doses once the blood culture's been taken.' He gave Wendy a compassionate glance. 'I'll try and get in early tomorrow morning just to see how she is, and if the mother's been able to give us any background medical history.' He pushed a hand through his hair wearily, looking at his wristwatch. 'I'm afraid I must go, Susy, but when Night Sister comes on tell her the mother may be in, and that Wendy needs to be kept warm and quiet. I'm sure she knows anyway.' He gave her a smile that lifted his mouth at the corners. 'Hopefully. See you at the party tomorrow, then.'

By the time Saturday morning had arrived, Susy and her friends had spent hours putting finishing touches to the food and drink for the big occasion. Electricians were fixing coloured lights around the garden, loud-speakers in the trees to relay pop music, and by midday everything was ready.

Shortly after nine that evening, the crowd from the hospital began to show up and Susy was not a little relieved that the house was in a comparatively isolated spot for such revelries. Julia and John had said that at the last count there were already some thirty people, and others still to come. Marc and Ross had swept in with still more, including Rebecca Cohen.

Marc handed Susy several bottles of wine. 'Happy birthday, from us all! We thought the hooch might help things along. I know we're in for a terrific evening. The weather's great, too!'

It was only then that Susy noticed Rebecca was draped on Ross's arm, as she smiled and said, 'If you want any help, darling, just yell!' Somewhat reluctantly, Rebecca freed Ross so that he could take a loaded tray from Susy, and carry it out to the patio. 'At your service, ma'am!' he grinned, his eyes skimming over her. 'And a very happy birthday from me to you!'

He made her feel beautiful, the way he looked at her. 'Thanks, Ross, so glad you could make it, and thank you so very much for the wonderful flowers.'

'A great pleasure.' He glanced behind him at a jostling group of exuberant young men. 'These young puppies came with me, I'm afraid!'

Susy immediately recognised Robert Sloan at the head of them vying for attention from her, while handing her a flamboyantly gift-wrapped box of chocolates.

'Even these wouldn't ruin that gorgeous figure, Susy!' he gushed, with a broad smile.

'Hi! Nice to see you, Robert! Thanks for the gift. I'll ration myself nevertheless!'

Guests continued to arrive. Dancing, eating and drinking soon turned the event into quite a bash, according to Hilary Mason, who seemed thoroughly content to help two of Susy's mother's friends in the kitchen in charge of food that needed special attention. Leaving the hive of industry, Susy caught sight of herself in the cream silk trousers and black bustier, yet she still felt overheated in the airless night. Or could it have been the Martinis she'd already had?

'Susy! There you are!' Ross called. 'The crowd wants to see you outside!' Birthday greetings, songs, good wishes and gifts were showered upon her. Afterwards she realised Ross was still holding her hand. 'What a great come-back you've made,' he was saying, looking at her admiringly. 'This party is celebrating a whole lot of things. Let's go back indoors and dance; at least the hall appears to be empty!'

'Great idea!' They did some mad disco dancing, showing off their prowess, until the rhythm switched and he took her in his arms; by that time they had been joined by several other couples.

'Back in the garden, I think,' he whispered against her ear. They glided through the hall, the dining-room, out across the patio, across the lawn and beneath the trees, where they stopped, and he looked into her eyes. For Susy, quite suddenly, heart beating against his, the rest of the world was eclipsed. Magically his lips burned against hers, and as if from a distance she heard him whisper, 'What better than a birthday kiss? Susy, you look wonderful tonight.' Voices could be heard coming across the lawn. 'I'll go and get us a drink,' he grinned, 'otherwise we might be misunderstood.'

She watched him walk off in his tall, elegant way, wondering if he had any idea what her thoughts were about him. She saw Ross, Rebecca and Robert Sloan bringing back a tray of drinks, everyone seemingly quite happy. Robert Sloan was at her side, slurring his speech slightly 'How are you, my darling? 'Another drink?'

'No, thanks, Robert.' He led her away from the others.

'This is your birthday party, Susy, make the most of it!'

'OK, then, but that's enough.' She sipped from the glass he'd given her. 'You were telling me you went to Morocco before taking the job this year?'

'Yes, I was there for six weeks. I have some great photos. I'll let you see them some time.'

'I'd like to,' she said absently, suddenly feeling quite woozy. 'I've been to Egypt, you know.' It was silly of him to be playing with her fingers, but she couldn't be bothered to pull her hand away.

'Terrific! That's the next place I hope to visit.'

'I have some pictures I could show you,' she laughed.

'Great. Let me see them.' He stroked her hair and nibbled her ear. 'You really turn me on, Susy. I'm firing on all cylinders.'

'Oh, let's go and sit down on the garden seat; I can't be bothered to go upstairs.'

He drew her head down on to his shoulder. 'I'd like it if we went upstairs.'

'Don't do that, Robert,' she giggled. 'Do you know what I think? You're too pushy,' her voice was slurred too, although she hardly realised it, 'and you kid yourself too much.'

'And I think you're very beautiful. Now, may I see those pictures?' His eyes smiled into hers. 'Please, just for Robert?'

She stood up, swaying slightly. 'You're a pest! Come on, then.'

In her bedroom she opened the door and flung a hand at the wall. 'Those sketches hanging there, I did them.'

He had closed the door behind her and sat down on the bed, drawing her with him. 'Come on, sweetheart, we can get a better view from here.'

'Hey, Robert! What the hell? Stop that at once!' His kisses suddenly got the better of him. In seconds her strapless top had been jerked from her breasts.

'Susy, Susy. . .' he moaned. 'You agreed to come, remember?'

'Let me go, you drunken oaf.' His hands were pulling at her trouser waistband, his body pinning her down. She couldn't move, and suddenly she felt very clear-headed, and began to fight back. 'Get out! Get out of my room before. . .' She thrust herself from under him, but he laughed, pressing her back to the pillows, his mouth wet and unpleasant over hers. She screamed out, twisting her head from him.

The bedroom door suddenly burst open and Ross stood there. In a quick glance he took in her bare breasts, her clothing half ripped from her. Robert scrambled off her, as Ross yanked him by the scruff of the neck and pulled him to his feet. 'Get outside! I'll talk to you later.'

'That's not fair, sir. We were. . .'

Ross practically catapulted him from the room. 'It's a pity I didn't let you damned well drown that day!'

Mortified, Susy sat up, pushing back her hair and adjusting her top, cheeks burning at her own stupidity as Ross said brusquely, 'It's your father and mother on the phone.'

'Oh, thanks, Ross. I didn't hear it, I'll take it up here.' What an utter idiot she'd been to act as she had.

His brow still looked like thunder. 'Are you OK?' he asked, with more tenderness than she felt she deserved.

'Yes, I'm all right, thanks.' She glanced away from him as she picked up the phone extension, placing her hand over the mouthpiece. 'I hope you didn't think I — ?'

He broke in, 'So long as there was no harm done, that's the main thing.' He left the room, still seething over that young fool, knowing somewhere deep in his heart that it wasn't something Susy would have organised, surely? Robert Sloan was going to get the benefit of his tongue any minute now.

Somehow, Susy finished the conversation with her parents, giving them all the news, and thrilled they were so delighted with their destination; a birthday present was on its way. Suddenly all the fuzziness had left her brain. Seeing Ross walk out as he had just now had cleared the last vestige of intoxication, if that was what it was, from her mind, leaving it only too sober. She straightened herself up and went downstairs, the party seemingly going on its merry way, the only change being that neither Ross nor Robert Sloan could be seen.

By dawn a barbecued breakfast was served, and when at last only Julia and herself were left to spend what remained of the night, they brewed masses of black coffee and talked and talked. Susy retelling the incident uppermost in her mind.

'Heaven only knows what Ross really thought, Julia. He must have left in a huff.'

'Don't be crazy, love, it wasn't your fault. Anyway, he probably wanted to tell Robert Sloan his fortune. I have a feeling that with such a bad start that idiot won't be with us at the hospital much longer. If I see him, I'll tell him the same.'

Susy sipped the coffee thoughtfully. 'Do you know, I still wonder if he put something in the last drink he gave me? I could kick myself, because for a while I could hardly think straight. I mean, not in a million years would I have taken him up to my bedroom.'

'Forget it! It was a terrific party, everyone said so, and I hope you live to be a hundred so that we can make it an annual event!'

Susy was back on duty early next day, and she was in charge. She just trusted to luck that nothing too dramatic happened on what should be a quiet Sunday. But as usual life kept a few nasty little surprises up its sleeve, and to her dismay she and the rest of the staff had only just finished seeing to the children, getting them bathed and fed, when footsteps sounded along the corridor and the office door opened and shut. Her heart raced; it was either the SNO, or Ross Beaumaris in a foul mood. She braced herself to go into the office, taking a deep breath as she did so and remembering to knock on the door. Her mind leapt ahead. Although she had only looked in at the party last night for a short time, the SNO had seemed her usual friendly self. It must be Ross. It was. His voice called her in.

'Good morning, Susy. This isn't a formal round; I just wanted a word about last night.'

She realised then that he was not on duty, that his cotton beige trousers and navy blue Guernsey over a blue and white checked shirt made him look far more approachable than at other times, too much so. Her heart lurched when she saw the quizzical look, nevertheless, in the searchlight eyes, conveying, she was sure, the belief that she had thrown herself at Robert Sloan with all the abandon of a baggage in his estimation. Swift colour rose to her cheeks guiltily, as she said in haste, 'Is it so important that you had to come in just for that?'

Ross caught the hint of sarcasm, and was still unable to forget his ready excuse when Marc was looking for her to dance with him, and Ross had said she was taking a five-minute break in her room. It was obvious Marc was in love with her, and he could have sworn Susy was with *him*. And what of Robert Sloan? Why should she have been taken in by such an apology for a man? Ross also found it impossible to put from his mind the monstrous tidal wave of rage that had swept through him when he'd seen Robert Sloan violate Susy's body: he had wanted to tear the man from limb to limb. Seeing her face at this moment, the anxious, but proudly stubborn look in her eyes, he cursed himself for his own thoughts about her; thoughts which, if he gave them their head, could mean he was going down the same road as with his ex-wife even though Susy was clearly an entirely different personality from her. Moreover, with Ian nurturing his daughter at every turn, heaven preserve him from nepotism yet again.

The soft colour had not subsided from Susy's cheeks as he said more curtly than he'd intended, 'Yes, it is important. I wanted to apologise for leaving last night when I did. Also I need to be certain you've had no ill effects after what happened.'

'I'm perfectly OK, thanks,' she answered, matching his tone.

'Look, I've one or two things I want to say, and there's not much chance here. Can we meet for dinner tonight?'

'Well, I was going to have an early night.'

'It needn't take too long.'

'Will six-thirty be too early?'

'No, fine. I'll pick you up,' he said, leaving her in no doubt as to what sort of date it was going to be.

After Susy went back to the ward, Ross remained seated briefly before going to the senior common-room for coffee; afterwards he intended going home as he was on call.

In the common-room, Marc strolled in and sat alongside him. 'Ross! I was hoping to find you here. I came in to say I have my tickets for the homeward trip. I'll be going back via Ireland. Gee, the time sure has flown. I have a couple more lectures and that's it.'

Ross's mind was still a whirlpool of his feelings for Susy—he wouldn't admit to love. Surely now was the time for a 'man to man' with Marc; at least he might get some idea whether he and Susy were planning a future together, especially as he was leaving so soon. 'Time really has telescoped, Marc,' he said with a wry smile. 'Still, great party last night.'

'Sure was! I had to leave before the barbecue, I'm afraid, but Susy's a great girl; she understood. She really deserved that party. In fact, she deserves a whole lot of things; I'd certainly like to be the one to give them to her.'

Ross felt a huge roar of jealousy explode within him, and it was with some difficulty that he said, trying to conceal his turbulent thoughts, 'Just what is it about you two, Marc? I mean, we're saying Susy's recovered now, but from what exactly, apart from a broken engagement? What's going on?'

His friend looked uncomfortable. 'Well, it's a little difficult, Ross. You see, only her parents, her best friend Julia and myself know.'

Ross thumped a balled fist on to his knee. 'For God's sake, know what, man? You can't get this far without telling me, surely?'

Marc's shrewd eyes summed up the situation. Ross

was in love with the girl and the poor devil didn't know where he was. He made up his mind suddenly. 'Look, Ross, this is confidential only because that's the way Susy wanted it, not because it's a state secret. You see, this young man of hers. . .' Marc went on to relate the entire happening, from the bomb explosion in Belfast to Susy's complete breakdown in hospital as a patient, then a psychiatric clinic, to her convalescent period, afterwards returning home to decide upon her future. 'Out of the tragedy,' Marc concluded, 'one of the biggest things worrying her was her ability or not to continue nursing, and. . .well, you know the rest. You do understand, old friend, this is completely between ourselves.'

Ross had listened with ever-increasing disgust at himself that he should have treated Susy the way he had at times. Filled with remorse, he vowed from now on to forget his earlier wrongful conclusions and comparisons with his ex-wife. As yet he still did not know for sure if Marc and Susy had anything going for them, and now certainly was not the time to mention it. He smiled at Marc ruefully. 'Thanks a lot, Marc; quite a few things are more obvious now. That poor girl has really gone through it. No wonder her parents were so protective; I have to admit at times I thought she was thoroughly spoilt, by her father particularly.'

'No, Ian is a tougher man than that.'

'I'm seeing her tonight for dinner, so if the subject comes up I'll tell her I'm to blame.'

'On your head be it! That young lady can fire off a few rockets when she likes,' Marc laughed, as they left the common-room together for the car park.

Susy wasn't too sure if she was looking forward to having dinner with Ross that night or not. Not only was he probably going to register disapproval about

Robert Sloan, but also she had a request to ask of him, and this meant telling the whole story about Patrick.

By the time Ross had picked her up, Susy had calmed down somewhat, yet prepared herself for a fairly humourless evening. They drove across from St John's Bay to St Brelade's and turned into the Old Portelet Inn. 'The food here is usually quite good,' he was saying, as they went inside. They were immediately shown to their table by an open window, the view out to sea dramatically enhanced by an indigo sky.

So far they had talked only in platitudes, and after the waiter had taken their order Ross leaned his forearms on the table, saying with some concern, 'You sure you're still OK being in your house alone, especially in view of one Robert Sloan?'

She resented the veiled implication that she couldn't look after herself.

'Well,' she said pertly, 'as for being alone in the house, I'm quite enjoying it. Regarding my physical survival, if you hadn't intervened on the night of the party, I dare say I would have coped.' A demon seemed to be perched on her shoulder as she went on recklessly, 'I don't happen to be a judo expert, but I know a few moves that would have saved me eventually. How do you know I wasn't secretly enjoying myself? You're not my keeper, you know, much as I appreciated your concern.'

His face hardened. 'In which case, you were not making it very clear,' he snapped. 'I assumed the fool was upstairs under false pretences.'

'I invited him, as a matter of fact, to see my Egyptian sketches.'

A small nerve quivered at his temple. 'Oh, come on! You're not that naïve, surely!' Controlled anger now hardened every word. His mind was reeling. Was this the beautiful, gentle girl he had heard about from Marc who had gone through so much? He hadn't been too

sure about inviting her out tonight, but the thoughts of
love that had beset his brain earlier were now rapidly
blocked. If it was Marc whom she loved, had *he* ever
seen this side of her, the calculating flirt which until
now had been disguised so well? He felt as if something
was breaking up inside him. The fact that Marc had
told him of her strength of will to come through all she
had, as well as reviving her career by her own efforts
to succeed, made him hardly able to believe this was
the same person.

He looked up suddenly to see her smiling, the brown
velvet eyes holding an expression that wrung his heart.
'Ross,' she whispered gently. 'I was only teasing, you
know, but you believed me. . .'

Suddenly the world was turning again, and he
relaxed, yet still did not understand her motives. She
certainly had the power to affect him more than he'd
ever thought possible. He smiled. 'Oh, dear, I was
caught out there.' A waiter was at their table. 'We'd
better talk later.'

They sat over coffee in the small, comfortable
lounge, the early hour as yet leaving them on their
own. She knew she had irritated him with her charade,
but she didn't see why he should carry on acting the
superior being when they were both off duty. She
settled back into her armchair, saying lightly, 'Ross,
before we go any further I must put the record straight
about Robert Sloan!' She told him of their first meeting
on her ward, when but for Julia he would have really
put her back up. 'At my party, I thought I'd try a
different tack as he was new with our crowd. He
seemed OK when he forgot his ego. We talked about
our travels, and I quite seriously invited him upstairs. I
agree that was stupid of me. But previously he'd
collected a drink for both of us, and later I actually
wondered if he'd put anything in it. I seemed unable to
think straight, my legs went, and everything went

woozy for a short while! I really do agree with you — he's a very unsavoury character. If he's not, he's going about things in a funny way.'

Ross looked ten years younger, then worried. 'Strange you should mention the drink; one of the other young housemen said something of the sort, but I thought it was just talk. In fact, that was one of the reasons I came down rather heavily on Sloan when I booted him from your room. I shall be keeping a very strict eye on that young man. At the first hint of drugs from now on, he's quite definitely out!'

'I hope I'm forgiven for my crazy pretence just now!' She smiled up at him beneath her lashes, a tantalising expression that illuminated her features. Her hair was highlighted by the soft lights behind her, and the dress she'd worn for the interview revealed her skin to be even more of a silken texture than the garment itself. 'I realise now how foolhardy it was to invite Robert to my room. Thinking about it another way, it could have been a certain bravado to prove that I was able to look after myself, but I reckoned without spiked drinks.'

He saw at that moment, despite the new knowledge he had about her, that she was not going to reveal all to him. She was still fighting back and wanting the least sympathy possible. His admiration for her was total and those first tentative stirrings of love for her had to be contained, still convinced as he was that Marc was the lucky man.

'Ross——' Susy moistened her lips, deciding now was the time to ask a favour of him much as she disliked doing so, but it was more important to her than anything else in the world. 'Ross,' she repeated, 'would it be OK for me to take this coming weekend off through to Tuesday?'

He looked startled at the sudden change of topic. 'Isn't this. . .rather unexpected?' The sharpness in his tone did not surprise her. Now he felt worse. Hadn't

Marc said he was going home via Ireland shortly? 'Is it that important?' he asked brusquely. 'Is there something worrying you?' He tried to conceal the true anxiety in his voice. Was she about to tell him now that, after all, she and Marc were in love?

Susy sat forward in her chair, hands clasped together as if to steady her emotions, a soft light in her eyes. 'Ross, there's something more I have to tell you. It's about my. . .my "broken" engagement. . .'

As Susy retold the tragic story, every word Marc had said was confirmed. In no way would he let her know that he and Marc had exchanged this knowledge; in fact his heart lifted at the thought that she had taken him into her confidence at last. Hearing it again from Susy only made it all the more poignant. 'So you see,' she concluded, 'I must go back to Belfast for Patrick's memorial service; his parents are expecting me. They have waited until certain relatives were able to come over, and now it's all arranged.'

He saw the memories in her eyes, the heartache she must have gone through and the stubborn determination to rebuild her life. He wanted beyond all else to hold her in his arms at that moment, to shield her from any more of life's storms. Despite his rising spirits when she began to tell him of all that had happened to her, slowly another, even more stark realisation was dawning upon him. Assuming that Marc and Susy were not in love, just as Marc had never truly got over losing his wife, and would not replace her, so Susy could well be the same with Patrick! Quite suddenly he panicked, was distraught, utterly helpless at the prospect of such a bleak and empty future without her. How could be possibly compete against a. . .dead man?

Susy's voice came through to him, and with difficulty he put his own selfish thoughts to one side. 'So that's about it, Ross. I just hope it won't inconvenience everyone too much at work.'

For a moment he looked at her, dark blue eyes filled
with compassion as tenderly he put a hand to the side
of her face, a gentle caress, which was all he could
allow himself to do. 'Susy, my dear, what a terrible
time you've had. All that you've said has given me
answers to so many things. I can see now particularly
why you wanted to handle it on your own. Nevertheless, your courage puts a lot of us to shame. Of course
you must go to Belfast for as long as it takes. It's going
to be another emotional strain upon you, and I don't
want you worrying about us back here.'

While they were talking further in general terms,
Ross's mind was being incisive with the true facts. Marc
would be there in Ireland. He and Susy were certainly
good friends and had suffered the same loss, so forming
an unbreakable bond between them. Ross knew he
himself had no role to play at this stage and must
perforce remain in the background, heart in mouth,
trusting that one day Susy might see him in a different
light.

Susy was saying, 'Thank you, Ross, it's very good of
you. Oh, yes, and I must go and see Robin before I
leave.'

He said with a quiet smile, 'Why don't we both take
the day off tomorrow and have him for the whole day?
I'll organise the staff rota with the SNO.'

Her eyes shone. 'Oh, Ross, could we? That would
be wonderful! But we mustn't forget Marc's farewell
party in the evening.'

'We'll have a liqueur now, and drink to all of that!'

Next morning with everything arranged, Ross picked
Susy up, then they collected a very excitable Robin.
He had a basket full of personal treasures: bucket and
spade, towel, teddy bear, mini-train, notebook, pencil
and ball, and was still waving madly to Matron until
they had already turned the corner out of the drive.

'Where are we going, Uncle Ross?' he demanded eagerly, from the comfort of the front passenger seat, so that, according to him, he could see everything before Susy.

'Well, Susy and I thought we'd tell you one place at a time, like dipping into a bran tub!'

'What's that?'

'It's a big tub with stuff like sawdust inside and you dip your hand in and pull out something nice!'

'That sounds great, Susy, doesn't it?'

Similar conversations took place along those lines for a good part of the day. First they visited a working steam museum, where Robin was nearly beside himself with joy at being held by the driver's mate and allowed to ride on a huge steamroller. Next there were icecreams and crisps, then they went to the Jersey Motor Museum where a rather ancient scarlet fire engine had Robin shrieking with delight at being carried all over it by a stalwart young man. Afterwards they had a special picnic down on the beach that Susy had prepared with his favourite foods, then they played ball games. A rest in the sunshine came before going to the Summer Show on the Esplanade, and Susy had never heard Robin laugh so much as he did at the antics of some of the comedians. Later, small souvenirs of the day were concealed in his basket, and they finished in a café eating baked beans and chips. 'This is my very favourite tea, Uncle Ross, although I like the things Susy makes, too.'

'I'm glad you said that, Robin!' Ross laughed. 'Do you know, you're one of the lucky ones? I haven't tasted any of those special things yet you told me about!'

Robin looked up at them both, saying solemnly, 'Well, you see, Uncle Ross, she loves me. I'm not sure if she loves you.'

Ross and Susy grinned at each other, although she

couldn't help a faint wave of colour flying to her cheeks. Ross added, as if to embarrass her all the more, 'Perhaps I should ask her, Robin, and see what she says!'

Robin was chasing a last bean around his plate, pondering on his own problems rather than answering Ross. 'I asked Susy if she'd be my mummy, but she said it's a bit difficult because she's not married.' He stopped as a thought struck him. 'She could marry you, Uncle Ross; I'd like that:'

Ross said with mock-seriousness, 'I shall have to think about that, too.'

'Well, *I* think it's time for us to leave, darling,' Susy said to Robin quickly. 'What a super outing we've had.'

Once Robin had been returned to the home, happily tired out, his chubby arms, freckled face, even his curls, touched by the sun that had shone for them all day, and goodbyes said, Ross dropped her at Rosebriar Cottage. 'I'll pick you up this evening for the party, Susy. Hope you're not too tired?'

'Not a bit; I loved it. You gave him a wonderful day, Ross; thank you.'

'Thank you, too. I think we both owe Robin another one like that for being such a great little chap!' He gave her a sideways glance. 'He certainly comes up with some original ideas!'

CHAPTER ELEVEN

MARC'S party was a mixture of both pleasure and pain for Susy. They had already decided to travel to Ireland together now that she had obtained leave, but thereafter the thought of his returning to the States was yet another wrench; part of hers and Patrick's past which she was to lose. Marc knew she and Ross had spent the day with Robin and was understanding when they made their apologies in order to leave early.

He grinned at them both affectionately. 'No goodbyes; we'll just make it "so long"! After all, you and I, Susy, will not come to the parting of the ways just yet, and you, my old friend——' he slapped Ross warmly on the shoulder '—will soon be coming over to the States to my hospital again; I'll have all the details fixed as soon as I get back.'

'That's terrific, Marc. Thanks for everything; your trip has been far too short for both of us.'

'Sure has. Look after Susy once I've left; there'll be no holding her back now that her career's set fair again! Isn't that so, honey?'

She nodded, not trusting herself to speak.

Marc flung an arm about her shoulders. 'Don't forget, now, we're never going to leave it this long again before we meet, and that goes for the both of you.'

Outside, a cool, fresh wind was blowing in off the sea, and Susy shivered. She hated goodbyes, more than ever now. In Ross's car they nudged their way out into the evening traffic; it was still light but heavy cloud was amassing as they left the town behind. 'We can certainly do with some rain,' Ross murmured, giving her

an anxious glance. 'Look, Susy, I was going to suggest
we had dinner out, but you must be tired and I can
understand how you feel about Marc leaving. His
friendship must mean a great deal to you.'

'It does, Ross.'

What else could she say? he asked himself sternly. It
was an established fact from their first meeting. An
everlasting tie that had arisen from facing death
together, helping others and not counting the cost to
themselves. A small glimmer of hope began to flicker
in his mind. Maybe he was too pessimistic. Perhaps in
Susy's own good time she could love again, and why
not him, provided he took it very slowly?

She was saying, 'Ross, I'll get something for us to
eat at home, shall I? We could talk there without
interruptions.'

His spirits rose another notch. 'Terrific idea.'

At Rosebriar Cottage the interior now exuded tranquillity and orderliness since the party. They closed the
front door on the light rain that had begun to fall with
the slow onset of dusk, and while Susy went into the
kitchen Ross found the small sitting-room and lit a fire
in the red-brick inglenook laid ready for such evenings.
A dark wine-red Afghan carpet, two large natural
linen-covered settees at right angles to the fire, a long,
low table, well-lined bookshelves and bowls of flowers
comprised the room. Ross made a salad and Susy
omelettes, and together they carried the trays back to
where the fire was sending gold spears of flame up the
chimney. They drank rosé wine with their meal and
listened to Mozart, Elgar and Segovia, having found
they had similar tastes in music. Susy, relaxed and at
her ease now with Ross, tidied the remnants of the
meal away with his help, then sat on the rug in the
fireglow, her back against the front of the settee. Ross
sat opposite, his long legs outstretched, head resting

back on the settee, eyes half closed as the glorious music cascaded softly about them.

When it ended, it hung upon the silence, reverberating around the room, until a burning log slipped and drew them back to reality. Ross sat up smiling. 'Ah, that treatment's better than aspirin any day!'

She nodded enthusiastically, knowing these moments would be with her for a very long time. She wished she knew what Ross's thoughts were. Was he pondering upon the relationship between Marc and herself? Not that it would be for any other reason than idle interest. Now he was gazing at her with an expression that still vaguely reminded her of Patrick; the firelight played on his features, his profile, and for the thousandth time she dwelt on why his wife had not tried harder with their marriage. Then the random thought took her down a more dangerous road, to the physical magnetism that still hovered between them, as far as she was concerned.

As now, it was as if just the two of them together in the room created its own sensuous presence. This was all wrong; she should never have suggested coming back here. She made to move suddenly from where she sat, but Ross was quicker. His eyes admired her, his blood pounded for her. With one sleek movement he was at her side, all previous resolutions forgotten. 'I didn't want you to do that, Susy,' he murmured. 'You look so desirable sitting there.'

He raised a supple hand to her cheek, his lips drawing closer to hers in natural progression, making her heart thud as if it would leap from her body. 'Susy, Susy, you drive a man mad.' The world began to spin. 'Your mouth is like a trembling flower, its petals unfolding to the warmth of mine.' Their lips met, her lips parted, his arms tightened around her as they fell back on to the carpet while he pushed a cushion beneath her head. They yielded body to body, his quivering and trembling against her. Ecstasy overcame her. It had been so long since she had been held by muscular arms, had felt a warm, gentle male hand caress her throat, tilting her head back, urging her into a submissive situation she could do nothing about, nor wanted to.

One madly passionate kiss followed another, the lean-muscled vibration of his body blended with hers. She was drifting away on a tide of sensuality from which there was no going back. Ross taking her to a pinnacle of sensation which she wanted to go on and on. His hand slipped inside the low neckline of her dress, teased her breasts, giving away the secret longings her body could not disguise.

'Susy,' he gasped hoarsely, 'you're so perfect, how can I. . .?'

From a far distance she heard her own voice, overwhelmed, as if in a dream-like trance. 'Patrick. . . darling. . .' Like a thunderbolt suddenly striking her, she realised with shocked horror exactly what she had said. 'Oh, my God. . .' She sat up. 'Ross, I'm so sorry; I didn't realise what I was. . .'

He had already moved from her, his voice low and expressionless. 'Forgive me, Susy, it was my fault; I should have known better.' He stood up, offering her a hand also, then pushed back his hair, straightening his tie. He gave a wry smile. 'Everything; you, the surroundings, the perfection—it was too much. I'm afraid I'm guilty of possessing all the puny weaknesses of a mere man; put it down to that, please. Am I forgiven?' His face was agonisingly tense.

In the soft lighting her hair was ruffled, velvety eyes luminous and sensual, her body attuned so perfectly to his, it was almost impossible to answer, except to whisper rather gauchely, 'There's nothing to forgive, Ross. . .' Her voice returned to something like normal. 'I'll make some coffee.'

He placed an arm around her shoulders. 'Let's go and make it together, then you can tell me about the arrangements you've made for the Belfast trip. Everything's organised — tickets, flight times and so on?' They went into the kitchen.

'Yes, all done.'

They sat at the table, and he looked into her eyes over the rim of his beaker. He had to know. 'I must ask you something, Susy; it's personal, but as I like to think we're good friends perhaps you won't mind. Are you and Marc. . .are you planning. . .? Do you love. . .?' He stumbled and stopped.

She touched his hand with a smile. 'Ross, as you've just said, you are my friend and I don't mind you asking this question; Marc is my friend too, as you know only too well. He's a good man and one whom I hope to have the privilege of knowing for a long time yet. As for anything else, no, I am not in love with him; he is still very much in love with his dead wife. I simply hold him in great affection.'

Ross's thoughts galloped wildly. So, in that case, he could be right, it could be that she was the same over Patrick, and, in view of what had happened when he was foolish enough to allow his feelings to get the better of him, highly likely. Yet he knew that he loved her; surely the nepotism angle meant nothing in comparison, certainly not now when there seemed little hope of her returning his love. Perhaps one day she might come to him of her own accord, but that was just a dream. Meanwhile there was the memorial service. All his instincts were that he must go too, look after her, protect her in some small measure from the deep well of sadness which was going to consume her for a while. Nevertheless, he had to let her go, entrust part of the time to Marc and his fatherly concern for the girl he so admired.

'Susy,' he said, 'are you sure you'll be OK on the

trip? You wouldn't want me to come, say, part of the
way with you?' He was relenting again; it just slipped
out, annoying him, yet proving that the joyous bitter-
sweet revelation of his love for her was already beginning to emerge once more against his will.

'Thanks, Ross. I'm going to be perfectly all right.
Patrick's parents and relatives will be there. I'm only
sorry my parents won't be.'

On Saturday morning Marc and Susy arrived at their
destination and parted company until the following
day, when the service was to be held at a small village
church on the outskirts of Belfast, to where Marc
would travel from his hotel. Patrick's parents had met
her and the love in their welcome was all she knew it
would be. That evening Father O'Hara came to the
house and had a few words with Susy, his philosophy
of life and death helping her to rise above the joy of
one and the sorrow of the other.

Next day the service was by no means sombre. In its
simplicity of praise and homage to Patrick and other
brave young men like him, Father O'Hara led the
congregation away from the prolonged grieving which
the Irish flower of youth would not want, but it would
always be a source of pride and love in bereaved
families that such bravery and dedication to duty was
what every man pledged who loved his country.

In a corner of the churchyard beneath tall, dark
green pines, the memorial stone to Patrick was a riot
of flowers. Before she left, alone for a few precious
moments, Susy said her first and last goodbyes to the
Patrick she knew and loved and who would remain in
her heart forever. She realised, too, as if he were
explaining it to her, that this now had to be the final
letting go, the end of one era and the beginning of
another. Father O'Hara's words were a poignant
reminder of it. 'Now you must go forward with your

life, my dear, find new directions. You have opened your heart to the children for whom you care, and what better start could there be than that? You must, as in the way of things, find love and happiness again. It is your birthright.'

When Susy returned home the following Tuesday evening, in less than a half an hour the phone rang. It was Ross.

'Susy! Welcome back.'

'Ross, you must be psychic! How did you manage it?'

'Premonition,' he laughed. 'No, I checked on your plane times and as you'd issued an ultimatum that no one was to meet you I thought I'd better stick to it.' His voice lowered slightly. 'Everything went well, I trust?'

'Perfectly, thank you, Ross. Marc saw me off at the airport, and sends you his best.'

'Fine. Now, there's a couple of snippets of news. Firstly from your parents; they'll be home on Saturday night, and I promised that you'd be at the airport to meet them. Hope you didn't mind me making your arrangements for you?' He felt like a schoolboy talking to her: excited, elated and still reeling with the prospect of seeing her again.

'That's great of you; of course I don't mind. And the second?'

There was a pause. 'Not quite so good. It's Robin.'

She caught her breath. 'Oh, Ross, what's happened?'

'Well, it seems when he couldn't see you — I went but that wasn't good enough — he asked for your mother, that wasn't possible, and he has gone into some quite frightening tantrums which really upset Matron, and that's saying something. At the weekend we hoped that going away with his prospective parents might help, but apparently it made matters worse.

They promptly brought him back, quite shattered that he was such a different child, and have practically decided to change their minds.'

'What do you put it down to, Ross?'

'Well, it's difficult; he's quieter now, but in an even more worrying way. He won't speak and refuses all food.'

'I'm not on duty until midday tomorrow, I'll arrange with Matron to go and see him,' she said immediately. 'Or do you think I shouldn't put in an appearance at this stage?' she added dubiously.

'No, I'm sure it'll help. You see, Sandra had gone away for the weekend, too, and we think Robin had convinced himself that she was never coming back again either.'

'Poor little soul. Perhaps I should go over tonight, right now?'

'No, let me talk to Matron first. . .' She heard another voice in the background, then Ross again. 'Sorry, Susy, I have to go. I'll drop in on my way home if that's OK?'

When he rang off, despite her anxiety she felt a small thrill of expectation at the thought of seeing him. Ross called in at the house in almost less time than it took for her to change from her travel-stained gear into something more presentable: jeans and the first shirt she could lay her hands on as the doorbell rang. She threw open the door, heart pounding, and there he was, a huge smile on his face, in a rather work-weary suit. He stepped inside, taking both her hands in his, a cheek-to-cheek embrace, and just very briefly when their eyes met she could hardly tear her gaze away, until she remembered Robin. 'It's so good to see you, Ross.'

'And you, Susy. I didn't get the chance to see Matron, but she rang me just now. If we can, she'd like us both to go over immediately. He's been sobbing uncontrollably until he could hardly get his breath, and he's under slight sedation at present, but Matron thinks perhaps when he sees us he may fall into a natural sleep. If, that is, you and I can console him.'

Nevertheless, as they arrived at the front entrance of the home, the entire place seemed quiet with a heavy sense of foreboding. Usually there was at least children's laughter or tears to be heard, but. . .

Matron hurried out to greet them, her face serious. 'I'm afraid Robin's now relapsed into what appears to be another bad bout of asthma. I may be wrong, Doctor, but I don't feel at all happy about him.' She showed them into a small room off the sick bay. Robin was lying in bed, eyes closed, forehead damp. 'He has this barking cough and hoarseness of voice which began last night,' the worried woman said. 'Now his respiratory and pulse-rate are up due to his fears and hysteria. The restlessness goes without saying.'

Ross nodded, looking with concern at the child. 'Yes, there's certainly a sign of a diminished amount of oxygen in the tissues. Unfortunately, exhaustion, or cyanosis, caused by circulatory failure, and the bluish tinge on the skin, must be regarded as an indication of trouble, I'm afraid. We'll get him into the hospital now. Susy, perhaps you'll stay with him in the ambulance and I'll drive on ahead.' He made a telephone call then left, saying briskly, 'I'll keep in touch, Mrs Harris, and thank you for what you've done.'

Once back at the peds unit in St Helier, the night sister, whom Susy had never met before, was quickly informed of the child's condition, and between them she and the pleasant woman, Sister Marsh, transferred Robin to Intensive Care and settled him with oxygen.

When Ross came in to look at the child's chest radiograph report, he frowned. 'Hmm, not too good; the infected lung has become quite solid and congested with blood, I'm afraid.' He glanced at Sister Marsh.

'He must have an injection of hydrocortisone immediately—serious measures for a serious situation, I'm
afraid. We can only hope now that the little chap still
has some fight left in him.'

Susy would never forget the following four nights as
long as she lived. Robin seemed to hover between life
and death, and she was sure it was simply that his
subconscious mind was still grappling with the deep
misery he'd been experiencing. She stayed with him
throughout the first forty-eight hours, alternating with
both Ross and Sister Marsh. Sometimes they talked
softly around his bed, in the hope that it might renew
some spark to hear familiar voices. The crisis point was
reached when suddenly his pulse-rate became a mere
flicker, his breathing almost non-existent. Desperate
that evening between the change-over between Sister
Marsh for Ross, Susy was alone for a few minutes and
sat on the bed, clasping the child in her arms.

'Robin. . . Robin. . .it's Susy!' she implored, willing
him to give some response. 'I'm here, darling; we're all
here to look after you.' Her tears would not allow her
to say more. Kissing him gently, she replaced the
racked little body back upon the pillows, burying her
head beside him, holding him fast to her as if to imbue
some of her own strength into him.

That was how Ross came in to find her. Sound asleep
out of sheer exhaustion. Her next recollection was
waking up on a couch in the office with Sister Marsh
standing over here. 'Come along, my dear,' she said
with a warm smile. 'You've had a couple of hours'
sleep to give you the energy to get off home now.'

Susy sat up. 'How's Robin?' she asked, not really
wanting to know the answer.

'Look, you just have this cup of coffee. Dr
Beaumaris said to tell him when you're awake. I'll ring
him now.'

Susy put her feet to the ground, finished the coffee

and straightened her hair. She stood up to glance from the window into the stygian darkness, for it was three in the morning. She couldn't bear the waiting. Ross was coming to tell her that Robin was dead. She just knew it. She loved that child like her own; nothing had proved it more decisively than when she had held him in her arms for the last time. She turned at a quick movement at the door. Ross came in, his face concerned. 'How are you now, Susy? You managed to get some sleep, thank heaven.'

'I'm OK, thanks, Ross, but Robin, is he. . .is he. . .?'

Ross's hands rested gently on her shoulders, his eyes looking deep into hers with compassion. 'My dear, I'm more than happy to tell you that after you left him last night his breathing became a little easier, his sleep more natural, the fever lessened. All infinitesimal pointers towards him turning the corner; the airflow obstruction is eased; and the crisis is over.'

'Oh, Ross, how wonderful.' She burst into tears of strain and relief.

'Isn't it just?' He smiled despite the tension on his own features. 'Isn't it just?' he repeated, tightening his hands upon her shoulders, kissing her tear-stained face. She knew it was an automatic reaction on both their parts, but at that moment she realised Ross had been at her side virtually ever since she came home. Could it mean that. . .? No. As they moved apart, she smiled, brushing the tears from her face as she looked up at him. Yet for herself she knew this had to be the new pathway to happiness Father O'Hara had told her to follow, the only one. Her love for Ross, for Robin, and the rest of the children with her job. How could she convey to Ross that she was freed now from all guilt and life-sapping grief, and that she loved him? The answer was that she couldn't. In these last awful days he had done as anybody would, particularly when the small boy meant so much to both of them. She could only steep herself in work.

In fact next day it was not difficult to do that. Wendy Moore was poorly. Susy had just given her one of the twice-daily injections of penicillin Ross had ordered to keep a constant level in the blood. Her leg was now immobilised in a plaster shell, and as Susy finished tidying her bedcovers she said with a smile, 'Your mum's coming in this morning, Wendy. 'Do you know what a little bird told me?'

Wendy, propped up with pillows, said aimlessly as she twisted a fair curl around her finger, 'No.'

'Well, it wasn't a little bird really, it was your mum, and she's going to change her job so that she can come in here every morning with you after breakfast and stay until lunchtime. Won't that be nice?'

'Yes.'

'She'll probably read to you, and play games, and. . .'

'I don't want to play games; I don't like them.'

'Well, there's another little boy in here named Robin; he doesn't like games much either, but he loves drawing. So how about me trying to get him to draw a picture of what he thinks you look like, then you can draw one of him?'

Wendy's face lit up. 'Oh, yes! Then I could send it to him!'

'That's a great idea! I'll go and tell him as soon as I've done the morning drinks.'

Hilary Mason was in the ward kitchen setting out the children's beakers. 'How's young Wendy, Susy? Ross was saying yesterday they might have to operate if the antibiotics don't penetrate that diseased bone.'

'Yes, we'll know in a fortnight. She's not too bad this morning, though—not quite so apathetic.'

'That's something, anyway.'

Susy still had a reasonably satisfied look on her face

as she drove home later that afternoon. Wendy's
recovery was going to be a long business, but hopefully
now, with the sheer joy of being back at the job, she
would one day see Wendy and many other children
leave the hospital to start a new life. Once indoors, she
had a phone call from Ross offering to take her to the
airport to meet her parents. When they all met up, it
was a happy foursome who had dinner out, though Ian
and Dorothy soon began to flag and were more than
ready for bed. Outside the house the two men tackled
the luggage, and Ian said suddenly, 'Ross, Susy looks
wonderful. That new job seems to have done the trick
for her, and, of course, she told us in her letters about
Patrick's memorial service, and what a greatly calming
effect it had upon her.'

Ross looked thoughtful. 'Yes, I think she's quite
back to her old self now. Eventually, as she's obviously
told you, she told me the whole story.'

Ian looked at him steadily. 'Yes, she wrote about
that too. I'm glad. Thank you also for helping to give
us our daughter back, Ross.' His voice shook slightly.
'We'll be eternally grateful.'

Ian's words seemed to reverberate in Ross's mind,
and that was when he was convinced finally that
nepotism had never been a part of Ian's plan. All he'd
wanted was to give a last desperate throw to pull Susy
from out of the terrible breakdown she had suffered.
The one remaining doubt in Ross's subconscious finally
left him. He clamped a hand on his friend's shoulder.
'She's a girl to be proud of, Ian, there's no doubt of
that.'

The following week saw small but steady improvement in Robin's recovery. He was now back in the
main ward, his wheelchair drawn up beside Wendy's
bed, and that particular morning Rosa and Susy had
just finished making his bed when Susy was called to
the office phone. For some unaccountable reason she

had felt low-spirited for the last few days. Maybe it was a reaction after all the high-flown declarations she'd made to herself about the future. Or was it that she'd hardly seen Ross and knew there was perhaps someone else? Rebecca Cohen. 'Orchid Ward,' she snapped into the receiver, 'Staff Nurse Frenais here.' Her heart sank; she must have sounded so waspish to Ross at the other end, but he didn't appear to have noticed. In fact he sounded decidedly cheerful. No doubt it was quite a relief to have her father back on the job while they were so short-staffed.

'Susy, when are you finished today?'

'Four o'clock.'

'Pity. I'm expecting some new equipment to be delivered between four and five. I'd rather like your opinion.'

'Well, I could hang on if it's essential.'

'OK, thanks. I'll be back by four then give you a ring.'

Susy immediately called Julia on Fraser. 'Hi—sorry, I can't make our swim after work. Ross wants me to give the once-over to some new medical aids. I suppose it's those bucket-top calipers and the extra Bohler-Braun frames he was cursing about that hadn't turned up.'

'Yes, but that's no reason why you should stay on after time, Frenais. Don't be too soft.'

'As if I would!' Susy laughed.

'OK, then, we'll make an arrangement later,' Julia said. 'I think our Rosso just wants to get you alone in the equipment-room!'

Just after four Susy went downstairs, Julia's crazy ideas having elevated her spirits, although she couldn't think why. She knocked on the door and went in. Ross put aside the letter he'd been reading. 'Ah, Susy; hope you didn't mind coming down?'

'Of course not.' She noticed there was no sign of new deliveries. 'Hasn't the stuff come, after all?'

He gave a huge smile. 'It certainly has. Just take a look at that!' He thrust a rather expensive-looking piece of stationery into her hand.

Puzzled, she read the gist of the formal note. 'We are pleased to inform you that delivery of. . .' She looked up at Ross with a frown, then at the letter again, reading aloud. '". . .a motor cruiser, *Pisces*, has been effected and will be berthed in the Yacht Marina, St Helier, C.I. to await your. . ."'

Susy was mystified. 'But Ross, apart from the fact this has nothing to do with medical aids, have you really bought another boat?' she asked wonderingly. 'A sea-going craft at that?'

'Indeed I have, Staff Nurse Frenais, and I'll tell you why.' He took the letter from her hand, still smiling, and she realised that in the true manner of a friend he wanted her advice. Her spirits flagged again, especially when he said seriously, 'Do you think Rebecca will like this? She's always on about weekends away.'

'I. . . I'm sure she'll love it. Well, I haven't seen it, of course, but. . .'

'No, that's the whole point of getting you down here for your opinion.'

'I can't do that; she's the one to approve it, surely.'

He shook his head stubbornly. 'No, you have to be the first to see it. Besides, there hasn't been much chance for us to talk lately; this is a good opportunity. I'll run you back to your place; you need jeans and a thick sweater.' He was in one of his arrogant, domineering moods.

'No, I. . .'

'Don't argue, woman! I also need to collect milk, sugar and coffee to entertain my first guest on board.'

Pisces was beautiful, shipshape in every way from stem to stern. 'Ross, it's marvellous, it's brand-new,' she gasped, stroking the immaculate rails, looking at the fenders, lifebelts. Down below was even more perfect. Two bunks, a tiny shower-room, galley, lockers for every conceivable thing. 'It all works, even tap water.'

'Come into the mini saloon; look, folding chairs, dining-table — you see? There; sit down, and tell me what you think.' His eyes were holding hers as he sat opposite her, the thrill of his new purchase lighting up his face.

She felt warm with embarrassment, even wearing only cotton shirt and jeans. It was an intrusion upon two other people's lives. 'Ross. . .it's perfect. I must go now. . .' She stood up, but he did the same, blocking her way, then he pulled her gently to him, an expression in his eyes that made her want to cup his dear face in her hands.

'Susy, forget Rebecca. It was just a ploy. I had to devise a scheme whereby I could get you to myself away from the world. By coincidence I'd ordered this craft a while ago. By the time it was near completion I decided this was the perfect way for us to get some very important matters sorted out. One of them to apologise to you for even daring to think that, as with Miriam, nepotism was stalking me again in the shape of your father and yourself.'

'Oh, but, Ross, that's just not true, I. . .'

He held up a hand. 'I know that now. I know too all the reasons why he acted as he did, and the fact that at times I treated you as I did shatters me just to think about it. There was the odd occasion also when I attempted to give an impression of being interested in Rebecca, just to put on some kind of macho act, I suppose. . . But, darling. . .'

The deep, loving inflexion in his voice made her hold her breath as he went on. 'Another of my faults — this isn't how I'd planned things. I didn't intend that you should know until I could be sure you were over Patrick. It's hellishly selfish of me. . .but. . . I love you so, Susy. Loved you for longer than even I realised, being so taken up as I was with my wrong conclusions.' He suddenly looked so unsure of himself. . .so lost. 'Could you. . .?' he stammered, clasping her hand. 'Oh, God, Susy, I'm putting this so badly. Is there any hope at all that you could love me? I'll wait forever if necessary.'

She was trembling with the miraculous enormity of his words. 'Ross, you said you loved me. . . I can't. . .'

Anguish created shadows on his face. 'Now I've made a complete fool of myself. I'm sorry. Honestly, I didn't dare to hope for any more than a possibility in the future for us. Believe me, girl, I wouldn't hurt you for the world.'

Suddenly she was in his arms, their lips met and she was vaguely aware that the floor beneath her was unsteady; it had to be Ross turning her legs into marshmallow again. He was showering tiny kisses upon her face with more apologies, the kind of kisses that could only happen in dreams. 'Ross. . . I was going to say I *can't* believe this is happening. You see, the memorial service and talking to Father O'Hara have taken away the awful guilty conscience I felt about ever loving anyone again. His words were that I must go forward. And oh, Ross, darling, I love you too. Ever since we met, I think! Remember the gooseberries?'

He grinned. 'Do I! And your gorgeous legs were stuck to the chair in the heat!'

'Ross, I feel so fit now in comparison to then.'

'You certainly look marvellous. But, darling, to think you love me. . .' he said, utter disbelief in his voice. 'Oh, Susy, Susy. . .' Suddenly they moved to one of the bunks, coffee forgotten.

'The floor's slipping away, Ross,' she murmured rapturously against his firm lips, their hearts together. Very slowly, very gently, he unbuttoned her shirt, as she did his. 'The whole world's slipping away, sweetheart,' he murmured passionately. 'My God, you are so beautiful.'

The floor was indeed tilting. Neither heard the quiet but inevitable lapping of the incoming tide against *Pisces'* newly painted sides, buoyed ever higher to the flood-tide of its natural cycle, as dusk settled over the harbour, while the sea engulfed the waiting shore.

Later, when a calm lay over the water, Ross and Susy were in each other's arms, ecstatically happy, but with Ross attempting to be practical. 'You see,' he said, at her question, 'the groceries we bought weren't necessary. I had Julia and Hilary rush to the supermarket for everything we needed tonight!'

Susy shot up. 'You mean they knew everything?'

He chuckled, saying against the tingling surface of her lips, 'No, not everything!'

She leaned on his broad, hard chest with a grin. 'I hope you don't think I'm Daddy's little girl any more!'

He gently urged her back on to the pillows, and sat up to lean over her, adoration in his eyes, a finger tracing the roseate contours of her face. 'My love, please forget that. You are the most beautiful and wondrous woman, the only one I shall ever want to love for the rest of my life. There'll be another Daddy's little girl one day after we're married — ours. Yes, and I almost forgot: why don't we organise a ready-made brother for her? Young Robin — what do you think?'

Thrilled at the suggestion, Susy placed her arms around his neck, the love in her voice giving him the answer. 'You are super. . .' she said slowly.

'So are you, and before we talk about wedding dates and honeymoon cruises to far-flung places I want to hear more about that English master who turned you on.'

'It wasn't. . . Well, I suppose it was! OK, I surrender, darling!'

SUMMER SPECIAL!

Four exciting new Romances for the price of three

Each Romance features British heroines and their encounters with dark and desirable Mediterranean men. *Plus, a free Elmlea recipe booklet inside every pack.*

So sit back and enjoy your sumptuous summer reading pack and indulge yourself with the free Elmlea recipe ideas.

Available July 1994   Price £5.70

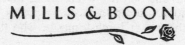

MILLS & BOON

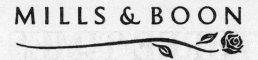

MILLS & BOON

LOVE ON CALL

The books for enjoyment this month are:

TROUBLED HEARTS Christine Adams
SUNLIGHT AND SHADOW Frances Crowne
PARTNERS IN PRIDE Drusilla Douglas
A TESTING TIME Meredith Webber

❤ ❤ ❤ ❤ ❤

Treats in store!

Watch next month for the following absorbing stories:

HEARTS OUT OF TIME Judith Ansell
THE DOCTOR'S DAUGHTER Margaret Barker
MIDNIGHT SUN Rebecca Lang
ONE CARING HEART Marion Lennox

LOVE ON CALL
4 FREE BOOKS AND 2 FREE GIFTS
F R O M   M I L L S   &   B O O N

Capture all the drama and emotion of a hectic medical world when you accept 4 Love on Call romances PLUS a cuddly teddy bear and a mystery gift - absolutely FREE and without obligation. And, if you choose, go on to enjoy 4 exciting Love on Call romances every month for only £1.80 each! Be sure to return the coupon below today to: Mills & Boon Reader Service, FREEPOST, PO Box 236, Croydon, Surrey CR9 9EL.

✂ — — — — — **NO STAMP REQUIRED** — — — — —

YES! Please rush me 4 FREE Love on Call books and 2 FREE gifts! Please also reserve me a Reader Service subscription, which means I can look forward to receiving 4 brand new Love on Call books for only £7.20 every month, postage and packing FREE. If I choose not to subscribe, I shall write to you within 10 days and still keep my FREE books and gifts. I may cancel or suspend my subscription at any time. I am over 18 years. Please write in BLOCK CAPITALS.

Ms/Mrs/Miss/Mr _____ EP63I

Address _____

_____

_____

Postcode _____ Signature _____

Offer closes 30th September 1994. The right is reserved to refuse an application and change the terms of this offer. One application per household. Offer not valid to current Love on Call subscribers. Offer valid only in UK and Eire. Overseas readers please write for details. Southern Africa write to IBS, Private Bag, X3010, Randburg, 2125, South Africa. You may be mailed with offers from other reputable companies as a result of this application. Please tick box if you would prefer not to receive such offers ☐